D0301910

# FINDING THE WAY

Debbie

Kope you enjoy

Alfred Wellnitz

3-23-2013

# FINDING THE WAY

Alfred Wellnitz

iUniverse, Inc.

New York Lincoln Shanghai

# Finding The Way

All Rights Reserved © 2004 by Alfred Wellnitz

No part of this book may be reproduced or transmitted in any form or by any means, graphic, electronic, or mechanical, including photocopying, recording, taping, or by any information storage retrieval system, without the written permission of the publisher.

iUniverse, Inc.

For information address:
iUniverse, Inc.
2021 Pine Lake Road, Suite 100
Lincoln, NE 68512
www.iuniverse.com

ISBN: 0-595-31590-9

Printed in the United States of America

# CONTENTS

▼

# CHAPTER 1

▼

# PRUSSIA 1871

He stepped off the train at Flatow into a cloudy, cool March day, wearing a blue Prussian uniform, carrying a rucksack that contained all of his personal belongings. Strands of reddish-brown hair protruded from under the edges of his cockade cap. A fledgling beard did not hide a youthful face with penetrating blue eyes, a face which appeared younger than his twenty-one years—certainly not the face of a veteran soldier. He was not a large man, but strength was indicated in the firm way he moved, in his erect posture.

There was no one to meet him at the train station when he arrived. This was as he expected. He had not communicated with his family for over two months.

Another person got off the train at Flatow, a young man Karl's age.

The man hailed him. "Herr Karl Mueller, remember me? Reverend Meyer's son, Martin."

"It's been awhile."

"So, back from the big war. For good?"

"For good. And you, back from somewhere?"

"Wittenberg, the university. My father would like me to follow his footsteps. I think the army might suit me better. How is your family?"

"Haven't heard for a while. Been moving around."

"Walk with me as far as the church. You can tell me about the war."

Karl shouldered his pack and the two walked towards the middle of the town exchanging news of their travels. For the most part, Karl deflected Martin's questions about the Franco- Prussian War. The experience of war, combat, the battle of Sedan, these were things Karl's mind had suppressed and it was reluctant to yield up those memories. Karl changed the subject to Martin and his current situation.

Martin expanded on the reason he was returning from Wittenberg. "I loved studying philosophy, things like that, but their application to religion is where I ran into a problem. The ministry and I don't seem to be compatible."

They were approaching a large church built with cut white stone. It had a towering square bell tower that was topped off with an oversized crucifix. The bell tower rose five levels above the street and was one of the tallest structures in the town. Beautiful stained-glass windows lined the sides of the oversized church. It was a Lutheran church built forty years previously to overshadow any Catholic church in the area—and it succeeded.

Martin turned off at a house beside the church that served as a parsonage. He waved to Karl, smiled and said, "See you in church."

Karl proceeded to walk to his family home located on the edge of the town. The home was soon in sight, a small cottage set off by itself near an open field. Karl noted the smoke coming from the chimney and imagined the fireplace and the room that it warmed in the only home he had known before being called into the army. His pace quickened as he anticipated being embraced by family and familiar surroundings.

As he drew nearer, he noticed some other people approach the cottage and enter it, and when he got to the door, he could hear the sound of voices within. As was his habit, he opened the door without knocking and found himself confronted by a room filled with neighbors, friends and relatives. The room was large, the only one on the lower level of the cottage except for a small bedroom in one corner. His mother and sister were sitting in chairs against the opposite wall next to a long wooden box that was balanced on two chairs. It was a coffin.

The presence of the young soldier standing in the open doorway with his rucksack at his feet was soon noticed. His oldest brother Walter and Johann, the next oldest, reached him first, grabbed and hugged him. They were followed by his mother Frieda and young sister Katrina.

"Karl, you have a beard!" Katrina exclaimed as she gave him a hug.

His mother put her arms around him and clung tightly. There were tears in her eyes, "Karl, Karl!"

"What's happening?"

She did not answer.

Walter answered for her. "Our father. It was sudden. Sorry you didn't know."

Karl was stunned. The image he had held of his family moments ago was suddenly changed. Rather than a homecoming welcome, he had walked into his father's funeral.

For Karl, sorrow was not an immediate reaction. Confusion was what he was feeling. Karl would have liked to turn around and walked out the door, to be by himself, to sort things out; but that was not possible.

Frederick, Karl's father, had dominated the family; he was *der Fuhrer*. It might not have always been in a positive way, but he was the leader. That structure was now gone, but the demands of the moment did not allow Karl to ponder how that would affect him or the family.

His mother continued to cling to him. It was not clear if she was expressing sorrow or joy, considering the circumstances. Other relatives and neighbors were now pressing to greet him.

Karl was greeted with unusual warmth. It seemed he was more of an attraction than the subject of the wake itself. It was not lost on these people that the Prussian Army had just achieved a stunning victory in France, and here in the flesh was one of the combatants.

Walter was asking, "Will you be one of the pallbearers? Herr Shultz was going to carry a corner, but you should be the one."

"Ya, of course."

The cottage where Karl's folks lived had served the family for over thirty years. It and all the land around it, and for that matter, all of the land around Flatow belonged to the Hohenzollern dynasty. Karl's father and family worked as peasants for one of the Hohenzollern estates, and use of the cottage was part of the compensation for the work they did. The Mueller family worked directly under one of the Hohenzollern *geschaftsfuhrers*. His name was Adolph Schaefer, and he had been the estate manager as long as Karl could remember.

A neighbor asked Walter if Adolph would be attending the funeral.

"I don't know."

"Well, he knows your Pa died, at least he should. I told him I was going to take the afternoon off to go to the funeral. Maybe he will come later."

"I don't think so."

"Ya, sure, Herr Schaefer has been a *geschaftsfuhrer* for so long he thinks he is a Hohenzollern. Not that we are short of people. A lot of people knew your Pa and besides that he made some of the best beer around. Tolerable wine. Can't blame them for wanting to test some of it. Not to mention all the food the Fraus brought."

Two farmers, helping themselves to the neighbor-furnished food and the deceased Frederick's beer, were discussing the departure of their neighbor.

"Died suddenly, working in the barn."

"Good way to go, don't you think?"

"Heart stopped; they say. Have you viewed him? Looks just like him."

"I need to do that."

"Ya, don't forget what we are here for."

The noise level increased as more attendees joined in conversations and as the sampling of Frederick's beer and wine continued.

Some of the young unattached women were eyeing Karl, who, standing erect in his uniform, seemed taller and more husky than his measurements would indicate.

A neighbor approached. "Karl, is your service time over?"

"Ya."

"What will you be doing, taking care of the Baron's fields again?"

"No, not that."

"What then?"

"I have plans."

Reverend Meyer had arrived. An average-sized man with no outstanding features, he used the office of pastor to set himself apart from the ordinary. He ran the church and congregation in strict accordance with the Evangelical Lutheran doctrine He would say a few words, then lead the procession out to the cemetery. He used a spoon to rap on the side of a glass to get the attention of those gathered. The room quieted: Reverend Meyer waited a moment for all of the attendees to focus on him. He then said a prayer for the family, one for the departed, and another for those gathered. That accomplished, he then sampled the food and the wine. After a reasonable interval, Reverend Meyer once more got the attention of the group and launched into a discourse regarding the departed. He started off citing the Gospel according to Saint Luke chapter 6 verse 2.

*And he lifted his eyes on his disciples, and said, blessed be ye poor, for yours is the kingdom of God.*

"Yes, blessed are the poor, for yours is the kingdom of God. Friends, we have lost a father, a husband, a neighbor; a good man. A man who lived a full life, and who had accomplished much. Frederick Mueller had no estate, was not a poet, a musician, nor a man of letters, or a holy man, but he accomplished much."

The pastor paused, looked about, then continued:

"What did Frederick accomplish, you may ask? You only have to look about and you will see three strong handsome sons and a lovely daughter, all of whom display outstanding characteristics. They are self-sufficient, hardworking individuals who have been brought up in the ways of the Lord. This is an outstanding attainment, shared with his grieving wife Frieda. This is what has been achieved. It is the greatest achievement that a man and woman can aspire to, and Frederick and his widow Frieda have succeeded gloriously in this effort. In this way of measuring, much has been accomplished.

"Families of great means and wealth, men or women with unusual abilities and talents may fail in this endeavor, a most important task for Christians on this earth.

"God is not impressed by the amount of gold or possessions one has accumulated or by a person's personal accomplishments. God is impressed by contributions to the Lord's family, the family of man, and to the future generations of the church."

Frieda and Katrina were weeping softly by this point while the sons maintained the expected stoic demeanor.

There was more from Reverend Meyer, much more. Karl could not help but wonder what had provoked the pastor down the path he'd taken. Whatever the reason, he was in fine form, and extended his remarks beyond what might seem reasonable for the occasion A number of the mourners, most of whom were standing, were becoming restless. The minister was interrupting the visiting, eating and drinking.

Finally Reverend Meyers completed his remarks. He paused long enough to drink another goblet of wine, then organized the procession to the cemetery. He would lead, followed by the pallbearers, then Frieda with her daughter, followed by the most immediate relatives, then the less immediate relatives, and last the friends and neighbors.

The mourners were wearing their Sunday best, as was Karl's mother, though she had added a black shawl, the only piece of mourning cloth that she could afford. The pall bearers had added black arm bands, the only variation from their normal Sunday dress. An exception was Karl, who wore the Prussian blue army uniform.

Karl, his two brothers, Walter and Johann, and a neighbor carried the wooden coffin with the remains of Frederick Mueller. The coffin was not heavy. The dead father had been a strong, stout man in his prime, but had shrunken considerably with age.

It was a cloudy day and there was a cold wind blowing from the direction of the Baltic Sea, driving a mixture of light rain and snow across the flat landscape. The small procession moved slowly down the muddy path toward the open grave that had been dug the day before by Karl's brothers. They reached the grave and the casket was set on two timbers that were laid across the top of the open pit. The procession broke apart and gathered about the grave site where the pastor once again held forth, but to the relief of the mourners chilled by the cold damp wind, he limited his remarks to only the essentials. He concluded by having the group recite the Lord's Prayer. He then commanded that the timbers be removed and Karl and the three other pallbearers, each holding onto one end of a rope, lowered the coffin into the shallow accumulation of water at the bottom of the pit. The pastor threw a handful of the wet, loose dirt on top of the coffin, pronouncing, "Dust to dust, ashes to ashes." The mourners dispersed while the three sons stayed to fill in the grave with the dirt recently dug from the earth.

Karl's thoughts were on the pastor's dissertation at the cottage, which had caused a mixed reaction in his mind. First there was the matter of his father's accomplishments, which were somewhat diminished in Karl's mind due to his greater knowledge of the details.

It was true that the children of Frederick were for the most part doing well. Walter, the oldest, was a tradesman. He had a successful butcher business, was married, and had recently become a father to a baby boy. Johann was a blacksmith's apprentice with only a year left to complete his internship. Katrina was a fine young woman, just turned seventeen, who should have no trouble finding a good husband. He himself might be a bit of a puzzle, but Karl was confident that his future would be successful. No drinkers or serious problems in the lot, but Karl wondered who should get the credit for that outcome.

Walter took a break from his shoveling to ask, "What did you think of the pastor's little sermon?"

Johann responded, "It was a bit long."

"But about what he said?"

Karl answered this time. "I hope at my funeral they don't say that all I accomplished was to raise a bunch of children."

"He was a peasant. What more could you hope for?" Johann asked.

Walter agreed. "That's true, hard work is all that you can be sure of if you are a peasant, and you will always have a little less than what you need. Sometimes we only had potatoes to eat, sometimes we didn't have decent clothes to wear, but I don't fault Pa for that. Every peasant family has those kinds of problems."

Johann mused, "Pa was strict, even mean. We all felt the whip and belt. I suppose this is a bad time to say it, but Pa was not a kind man."

Bringing up the father's faults as the three sons were filling his grave did seem like bad timing, but Walter had opened a wound and the three sons went on to purge it.

"Ya," Walter remembered. "He treated us pretty rough until we were big enough to challenge him. Poor Ma never got that big."

Karl had taken his share of abuse, but that was not all that troubled him. "Pastor Meyer had it wrong on a number of counts, as far as I'm concerned. That the family turned out pretty good was due to Ma, that's what I think. Ma is the one that made sure we all knew how to read and write, do numbers. Pa didn't have time for that, but thought he knew everything there was to know. But you are right about the things we didn't have. Pa worked hard, that is for sure, didn't waste things. But for me, I don't want to die owing much and owning nothing. If I work hard all my life, like Pa did, I would hope to do better than that."

Walter acted surprised. "That is big talk for a little brother. Sure you would like to do better, we all would, but sometimes it's easier to say than do."

Karl agreed. "In Flatow, it would be hard. But I talked to men in the army that plan to go to America. Work hard and smart, and you have as good a chance as anyone. You don't have to be born right, like here. Because I'm Frederick's son, I have limits. I and everyone else knows that. I'm going to America. In America everyone has a chance to be what he can be."

"Going to America!" Walter exclaimed. "Are you sure? That place is a wilderness. They are fighting with the Indians all the time."

Karl was warming to his subject. "Many German people are going to America. In America you can become the owner of land, just by claiming it and living and working on it. There are no peasants, no counts or barons, no Adolphs. You should all come with me. There is room for everyone."

Walter demurred. "I have a business, a family. Why give that up for something I don't know, thousands of miles away, completely cut off from what I do know? Maybe for you Karl, that is all right, but for me, no, that is not a good idea. I can tell you that."

To Johann, the idea was more interesting. "Karl, do you think they could use a blacksmith in America?"

"They can use everything," answered Karl, not knowing for sure, but the possibility of his brother joining him was reason enough for a positive answer.

Johann dug his shovel into the dirt and continued, "That is something to think about, but first I have to finish my apprenticeship."

The conversation about their father had left Karl feeling guilty. The man being criticized was in the coffin they were covering with dirt. Whatever his faults, this was not a good time to discuss them. Yes, Walter had led them into this conversation, but Karl had jumped in willingly, helping take it into the direction it had gone. Despite their father's faults, or maybe because of them, Karl did feel grief for this imperfect man who had left them. There is loss in death, there is no other way to figure it, and Karl was feeling the loss. The misty rain hid tears that welled up in his eyes, and he felt a need to wipe his nose.

The three brothers finished filling the grave, picked up their tools, and headed back to the cottage where their mother, sister, and Walter's wife would be waiting and where they would eat supper.

*     *     *     *

At the burial site, Karl had described to his brothers his plan to emigrate to America for the first time. It was a plan that had developed and taken form while he served in the army.

Being required to serve in the army had been traumatic. That period in Karl's life had changed him in ways that even he did not understand. The world that he knew had been enlarged. He had seen places and people that he had not been aware of and was trained to do things which he had never imagined himself capable of doing. The army experience also opened his mind to possibilities that he had not considered before. He had been part of a unit of twenty men who, through training and finally combat; had become like a family. They were like brothers. They shared many things, including their plans for the future. A number of the men talked about emigrating to America, where they said there were unheard of opportunities for ordinary men. Karl's best friend Hans had planned to emigrate to a place called Omaha, where his sister and brother-in-law lived. Hans had planned to start from there and then homestead land in America. Hans wanted Karl to join him, and Karl had agreed to do that. At Sedan, half the men in his unit were killed, including Hans. After recovering from the distress of battle, Karl decided that he would still go to Omaha, and eventually homestead land in America.

There had been concerns about his plan to go to America. There were concerns about the funds he would need to get to America, the approvals, concerns about leaving his family and the community where he had spent his young life.

He reached into the pockets of his army coat, and felt the solution to his money problem. Sewn into the lining inside the pockets were seventy two thalers. It was money collected when he was discharged, money that had accumulated in an account kept by the army in his name. Karl had only drawn a small portion of his pay while in the army, knowing that whatever he drew out would be spent in one way or another. He hadn't been saving for any purpose, but now it would pay for his ticket to America. He had heard that passage on a ship cost fifty thalers, and it seemed reasonable to assume that he could get to Omaha with twenty-two more.

Now there was another concern—his mother and her welfare. What would happen to his mother if he left? If Karl did not stay and work for the Hohenzollern estates, as he had before he went into the army, she would likely be turned out of the cottage she now lived in. His family would be replaced by a younger family that would be more useful.

That was one problem. Another was that Frederick had died leaving no estate, but leaving debts in the form of advances by the Hohenzollern estate. Debts to be paid by services to be provided by his family.

If Karl left, and did not work for the estate, it was not clear how that debt would be repaid. Karl's mother worked in the Hohenzollern mansion, two kilometers across the field from the cottage, but she earned so little that it would take forever to pay the debt. The seventy two thalers sewn into his coat could help settle the debt, but that would be the end of his dream to emigrate to America.

Karl loved his mother. She would do anything she could to help her children. Now she needed help, and Karl could provide that help. How could he even consider not doing whatever he could when she had this need?

# CHAPTER 2

▼

# THE FINAL DECISION

Walter's family would be joining the rest of the family at the cottage for dinner the Sunday after the funeral. Karl walked his mother to and from church that morning. On the way back he asked what her plans were.

"What is there to plan? I will work, still clean at the mansion, work in the fields during busy times, like always."

There was no indication of doubt in her words or demeanor. That what she anticipated depended upon Karl's acceptance of his role in the plan was not a concern.

Frieda's appearance was typical of older peasant women. Plain, with a strong, stocky figure and a face and hands that showed the effects of many days spent in the fields. As the wife of a peasant, her life had not been easy. She had known hardship and hard work and abuse on a first-hand basis. However, as a mother, she had not been typical. For most peasant women, having babies, lots of them, and feeding and clothing them was the extent of motherhood. For Frieda, motherhood extended beyond that. Karl recalled from as early as he could remember that there were regular lessons in reading, writing and numbers that Frieda would oversee. Lessons which lasted until he was able to read the Bible without assistance, write a letter, and do his number tables.

His mother continued to talk as they made their way back to the cottage. "Herr Shaffer will be glad to see you back. He likes you, he told me that. He knows you work hard and do a good job. Warm weather is coming and it is good to have you back. I missed you, we all missed you. When the war started I was afraid, but now you are back and we are going to have a good spring."

When they arrived at the house, Walter's wife and Katrina were preparing dinner. Frieda joined them.

Food smells, pungent sauerkraut and spicy *wurst* spitting in the pan, filled the cottage. The men tapped one of Frederick's kegs.

"Pa made the best beer around," Walter acknowledged as he filled his mug with the golden fluid.

Johann raised his mug in salute. "I'll drink to that." Then, turning to Karl he added, "and to your America plans."

"How soon would you be going?" Walter asked.

"If I go, it will be as soon as possible, in a month or two."

"That soon?"

"Ya."

"What do you mean by "if"?"

"There is a lot to think about, Pa passing away…"

Dinner was ready and they all seated themselves around the large dinner table. The simple Lutheran meal prayer was spoken in unison.

*Come Lord Jesus*
*Be our guest*
*Let thy gifts*
*To us be blest*
*Amen*

It was not a feast, but a good meal. In addition to the sizzling hot *wurst* cut into bite-size portions and steaming sauerkraut, there were boiled *kartoffel* and heavy black *brot*. There was also a special treat, apple strudel made from what was the last of the previous fall's apples.

There was small talk while the serving plates were passed.

Johann mentioned that Martin, the minister's son, had quit the university and was coming back home.

Karl remembered, "Ya, I met him at the station when I got off the train. What is he going to do now?"

Johann laughed. "Drink."

They all laughed. It was general knowledge that Martin liked his nips.

After a while they got to a subject that was starting to raise questions in the minds of most of the family.

Walter brought up the subject. "Ma, I suppose you haven't had much time to think about it, but do you know if you are going to make any changes?"

"Life goes on. I will do what I always have."

"What if Herr Schaefer won't let you live in the cottage?" asked Johann.

"Of course I will live here. Where else would I live?"

Walter was sorry he had brought up the subject, but it was too late. It had been brought up and Frieda's certainty was not shared by all at the table.

"Karl is back," Frieda stated. "Herr Schaefer likes him, will want him to work on the estate."

Katrina agreed, "That's right, Adolph likes Karl."

"But Karl, do you want to work for Adolph?" Johann asked.

Karl looked uncomfortable and did not answer.

"You told us, on the day of the funeral, that you were planning to emigrate to America and claim some land."

Frieda gave a little gasp. "Is that so?"

What Karl had been avoiding was now out in the open; he could no longer ignore it.

"That is what I was planning," Karl conceded. "A person I met in the army, Hans, was planning to do that, and he convinced me that I should join him. There were others in the army who said they were going to America. There is work for everyone, land for anyone who wants it. It sounds too good to be true, but they were all saying the same thing. I don't have that kind of opportunity here. I made up my mind that I would go. Now I'm not so sure. Pa dying has changed things."

Frieda voiced her concerns. "If you leave, Karl, you will be gone, you will disappear across that ocean. I know, that's what happens. If you leave, I couldn't live here. Herr Schaefer would want someone living here who is working the estate's fields…" Her voice trailed off.

Karl knew she was right. If he left, his mother would have to leave the home where she had lived for thirty years, the place where all her children had been born and raised. If he stayed and worked the estate's fields, there was little doubt in his mind that his mother could stay in the cottage. Was it too much to expect, for him to help her when she had this need? Everything would be so simple if he stayed in Prussia.

There was an uncomfortable silence around the table. It was apparent to everyone that Karl held the key to Frieda's immediate future and that her plans depended on him. Karl would have to make a choice and there was conflict involved in whatever choice he made.

Walter had been listening to the conversation and observing the reactions around the table. Finally he spoke. "Ma, things have changed, things are going to change, we can't keep things like they were, and if we could, we wouldn't want to. If Karl stays, he would be a peasant the rest of his life working for the Hohenzollern estate. If you think about it, you wouldn't want that. If the choice is to be a peasant in Prussia, or go to America, the answer is easy. Karl should go to America, if that is what he wants to do. We will work out what is best for you, as best we can, you can be sure of that."

Walter, the oldest son, the new head of the family, had spoken. What he proposed would be difficult for his mother, but sometimes there are no painless choices. Karl was free to pursue his dream, and the family would deal with the consequences.

# CHAPTER 3

▼

# THE FIRST STEP

The decision had been made, and now Karl needed to work on the details. First he needed to go to the city hall where all affairs between local Prussian citizens and the government authorities were conducted.

Karl entered the city hall for the first time since he had registered for military service. He found the city registrar's office where the government kept records of births, death, and marriages and processed people being inducted in the army, or who wanted to emigrate.

Karl was greeted by Herr Schmidt, the same bureaucrat that had helped him with his military service induction. Herr Schmidt had been around for as long as Karl could remember and knew everybody in the town.

"Sorry to hear about your father. You finished with your service time?"

Karl nodded affirmatively.

"What can I do for you today?"

Karl told him he wanted to emigrate.

"You want to emigrate! Leave our province, its beautiful lakes and forests, leave your family? Well, you aren't alone, have been getting a lot of requests. Where are they putting all of them?"

"It's a big country."

"Must be. There are forms you have to fill out. You read and write, don't you?"

"Ya."

"You should be able to figure these out yourself. When do you want to leave?"

"As soon as possible."

"Well, get those forms back. There are ships sailing every week, almost every day in the summer. Fare is about fifty thalers. There is a question on the forms about why you want to leave. Don't say you want to get out from under the Hohenzollerns, or to get away from fighting Bismarck's wars. Those are wrong answers. Say something like you are going to join relatives, you have work waiting for you somewhere, something like that."

"I plan to homestead some land."

"That should work, I have seen that used before What does that mean anyway, 'homestead'?"

"You put your claim on some land, don't cost you anything, live on it, work it for five years, and it's yours, sixty-five hectares."

"Good land?"

"You pick it out."

"For sure, that is tempting."

Karl filled out the forms, turned them into the registrar's office, waited for permission to emigrate. Field work had started. No one had told Adolph that Karl was planning to leave, so Karl went to work in the fields as though nothing was going to change.

Karl found himself caught up in the optimism that seemed to affect all men of the soil in early spring. They were anxious to work the land and plant the seeds in the perpetual hope that this growing season would result in a perfect harvest. Although every season brought its own set of disappointments, hope at the beginning was always high. Rains would be timely, there would be adequate sunshine, and plant pests and diseases would not spoil the harvest.

Distracted as Karl was by his plans for the future, they did not suppress the urge he felt to work the fields and plant the new crop. He spent his days in the company of a pair of fine chestnut Belgians, stirring the ground and preparing the fields for planting oats and barley. Adolph was a fancier of fine horses and managed to keep an attractive stock of draft animals on the estate he managed. The Belgians, a new breed line, had recently been imported from France to enhance the estate's horse herd. Adolph showed a measure of trust in Karl when he let him use these prized animals.

Karl would miss working these fields, miss watching the passage of the seasons and the familiar scenery. If this land and these horses were his own, there would be no need to look elsewhere. He would be satisfied to settle down in this place he knew so well. But that was not to be, and so he prepared to cross an ocean and half a continent in an attempt to find something similar that would be his own. He would certainly miss his mother and the rest of the family, but the promise of free land, unlimited opportunity, and adventure overwhelmed the ties that bound him.

On the first day of June Karl received word that all of his papers were in order and approved. Most ships left from Hamburg or Bremen. Herr Schmidt recommended going to Bremen.

"Ships leave there almost every day in the summertime. They will put you on the first one that has room. Should not have to wait more than a week in any case."

"That is long enough. I can't afford to sit in Bremen very long."

"You shouldn't have to."

Karl made his final plans and packed the small steamer trunk that would carry all of the worldly goods that he would take with him. This included two changes of clothes, two towels, two bars of soap, a razor, scissors, a pair of gloves, a cap, an extra pair of shoes, a light jacket, his army coat, and a light blanket. He also packed his confirmation Bible and Lutheran Small Catechism.

The family gathered the night before he was to leave by train for Bremen.

Karl and the family knew that once he left Flatow, they would likely never see or hear from him again. So his parting was not celebrated. This was *auf wiedersehen*, good-bye, not "until we meet again," but good-bye most likely forever.

They drank some of the remaining beer that Frederick had brewed. Walter suggested that it could be a long time before he tasted better beer.

Karl agreed. "It isn't easy to leave, especially after working in the fields the past few weeks. I will miss that, but what is pulling me is stronger than what is holding me. I'm anxious to get on my way."

Walter laughed. "Young men are always itching to find out what is on the other side of the hill."

His mother had reluctantly accepted the fact that Karl was leaving. She had dried her tears, but she still had one concern.

"Karl, how will you find a good German Lutheran woman in that faraway place?"

"I hadn't thought about that."

"Well, it is something you should think about."

"Maybe I will find an Indian squaw and convert her."

"You wouldn't!"

"Ma, if that is the biggest problem I have, you shouldn't be worried."

They drank the last of the beer, Walter and his family said their good-byes, and they all turned in for the night.

The next morning his mother fixed his breakfast and found she still had a few more tears when she and Katrina hugged Karl for the last time.

Karl walked to the train station with the sea trunk on his shoulder, got on the train, and left for Bremen. He looked back through the train's windows until he couldn't see Flatow any longer.

# CHAPTER 4

▼

# THE VOYAGE

In Bremen, Karl found his way to the office where passage on the ships of the North German Lloyd ship line could be purchased.

The ticket agent checked a ledger, "Space left on SS *Ohio*, leaving in two days."

Karl would not have to tarry in Bremen.

On June 10, 1871, Karl joined a large crowd gathered at the dock where the SS *Ohio* was tied up. The crowd was made up of Germans who originated from Bavaria, Saxony and Prussia for the most part. Karl was glad to see there were no sails on the masts of the SS *Ohio*, which told him it was powered solely by steam and was a newer ship.

When the loading started, the passengers were separated from their sea trunks. Each person was allowed to keep only as many personal items as they would need for the voyage and could carry in their arms or in a small valise or sack. For Karl, this amounted to his coat, a clean change of clothes, a blanket, a towel, and a bar of soap. Other men were carrying enough schnapps to last the entire trip, and some, not trusting the ship's galley, packed as much food as they could carry. Women with babies carried bundles of baby supplies in addition to their personal items. The people were directed to move up the gangplank to the main deck where they commenced to mill about. Each passenger had been given a ticket which specified the compartment to which they were assigned; unfortunately it seemed that none of the passengers had any idea how to connect the ticket information with an actual location on the ship. A few leather-lunged crewmen were shouting instructions to the bewildered emigrants as they tried to bring order out of confusion. A harried sailor looked at Karl's ticket and pointed at a hatch. "In there, down three levels."

Following others, Karl descended through further confusion in the passage-ways until he came to what seemed to be the bottom of the ship where he entered a compartment dimly lit by oil lamps. It was a space with three tiers of bunks lining each side and another row of bunks running down the middle. Karl's eyes adjusted to the dim light. There was a space a yard wide between each row of bunks and two and a half feet of headroom above each bunk. Near the entry were two tables measuring four by six feet. Karl found the spot identified by his ticket, number 25, Aft Compartment. It was a middle bunk on a side wall.

He started setting up housekeeping, arranging his meager personal items. There was a straw tick and a blanket, but no pillow, so he arranged his change of clothes and coat to make one. When Karl was putting the finishing touches on his bunk arrangement, he felt a slap on his back.

"Looks like we will be neighbors. I'm right above you. Heinrich is the name."

Karl turned and saw a gangly young man about his age, roughly the same height, with wavy brown hair that needed cutting. On the man's face was a smile and the start of a ragged beard.

Karl introduced himself. "Herr Karl Mueller, from Flatow, West Prussia."

"I won't hold that against you."

"Heinrich is your last name?"

"That is sort of a mystery, but I use Schlicter. Herr Heinrich Schlicter if you want to be formal."

"You don't know?"

"I didn't have a father."

"That is a mystery for sure."

There was hardly room to move in the narrow spaces between the bunks which were now jammed with men, mostly young, all trying to get settled in this bizarre place. It seemed like the compartment could not hold more people, but more kept pressing into it. Before everyone was fully settled, movement could be felt. The ship was underway. The stagnant air was filling with pipe smoke and the smell of over a hundred men. This would be their home for the next two weeks.

Crewmen came in with two boxes which they sat on the compartment tables. They issued a metal cup, plate and bowl and a knife, fork and spoon to each person—theirs to keep until the end of the voyage.

After the utensils and dinnerware had been distributed, the men were informed that meals were served in the mess one level up. Their compartment ate at 7 a.m., 12:20 p.m., and 6 p.m. They would have twenty minutes to eat. The latrine was on the same level as the mess.

It was approaching 12:20 p.m., so the men crowded up the passageway to the next level where they found the mess being cleared of a mixed group of men, women and children.

There were eight twenty foot long tables in the mess, with ten stools along each side of each table. Everything was bolted to the deck. Each table had a railing at one end, four inches high, that kept a a large pot of coffee, a basket of bread, and a container of soup from sliding around. The men filled their bowls with the watery potato soup, helped themselves to the hard, dry, dark bread and lukewarm coffee.

Karl and Heinrich sat down together to eat.

Karl observed that the food was meager and tasteless.

Heinrich agreed, but said it was a lucky thing. "Being tasteless makes it seem less meager."

Karl had to admit there was some merit in that. "Guess for fifty thalors we shouldn't be expecting a banquet served on china."

Karl had never been at sea before, and feared the plague of seasickness that was common for first time seafarers. He was not encouraged by how much the ship rolled in what was apparently a calm sea. They had been underway only a few hours when Karl began to feel nauseated, but he found that lying in his bunk and closing his eyes calmed him.

Lying still steadied Karl's equilibrium. It relaxed his body and allowed him to reflect on what was happening. The past few days had been hectic and there was little time to do anything but react to whatever the circumstances were that he was encountering. Now, as he lay still in his bunk, he could feel the pulsing of the ship which was relentlessly moving him away from what had been his home and what was familiar towards what he could only imagine. Images of his family and of lanes and fields that he would never see again filled his consciousness. Karl did not attempt to divert his mind from these nostalgic wanderings which seemed to sooth him. He remembered the tulips and daffodils blooming earlier this spring, and the fragrance of flowering apple trees. Memories of the cottage that was his home, and of his mother and family filled his head. The likelihood that he would never see them again disturbed his thoughts and he was suddenly overwhelmed by a feeling of sadness and loneliness. He could sense tears welling up in his eyes and running down his cheeks. Though invisible in the poorly lit room, he felt embarrassed and wiped the tears with the back of his hand. He fell into a fitful sleep, despite the sounds of a hundred men coughing, snoring, and getting into or out of their bunk beds, and his own uneasiness.

Towards dawn the ship began rolling further from side to side. Added to this was a steep pitching fore and aft. The ship groaned and creaked and the ship's screw, located not too far aft of their compartment, could be heard to rev up when it was tossed up and out of the sea. It was apparent that the ship had encountered heavy seas—a storm. This chaotic motion, combined with the crowding and growing stench caused by early victims of motion sickness, set off an epidemic.

Karl lay in his bunk, listening to the commotion. Closing his eyes and trying to relax could no longer overcome the rising nausea he was feeling. He made it out of his bunk and onto the pitching deck, slippery from the results of previous seasickness victims, but got no further. Heinrich, in the bunk above him, did not make it that far. The shadowy, under-ventilated, poorly-lit compartment reeked. Karl succumbed to the ravages of motion sickness. Never had Karl been so miserable. The nausea, the filth, the stench, were overwhelming. The time of day, whether it was night or day was not clear, nor did it matter.

After what seemed like days there was a detectable change. The nausea that had been gripping Karl subsided, and the ship did not seem to be rolling and pitching as much. Karl and many of the other compartment occupants were finding their sea legs. Conditions began to slowly improve. The compartment was cleaned and life became a little more bearable.

Heinrich had also recovered and was getting back to normal. He was able to find something positive about the episode—he couldn't eat the food being served in the mess.

Karl carefully packed tobacco into his pipe and lit it. "That was a blessing alright. For every bad thing there is something good. I think there is a law about that."

Heinrich frowned. "What about all this smoking? What is good about it? One can hardly breathe."

Karl took a puff. "It's something to do."

"Think of something else. What about challenging the pinochle champs?"

A perpetual pinochle game was being played at one of the tables in the compartment. The winners of a hand got to stay at the table, while the losing players were replaced by challengers lined up to take on the winners. Karl and Heinrich got in line to challenge the winning players.

A knot of kibitzers and gossipers hung around the card game. A favorite topic was how bad the conditions were on the ship. "Things are bad but could be worse," one passenger advised. "You could be in a family compartment."

"Ya, I heard that was worse."

Another man in the compartment joined in. "Maybe you will be lucky. Get sent back. Get to ride an empty ship back, at no cost to you."

Someone asked, "What do you mean, get sent back?"

"They take the dirty, the ignorant, the tick-infested, but not the lame or sick. If you limp, hack, or run a fever, you get a free ride back. If it is a child under twelve, someone has to go back with it."

"An inspector, a medical person, looked at everyone coming on the ship before we left."

"He fills a job and draws a salary. The real inspection is when you dock."

The current pinochle champs disposed of another set of challengers and it was Karl and Heinrich's turn to take them on. The cards, worn and dogeared, were dealt. They were playing with a double deck and the dealer announced that five hundred was the minimum bid. Karl shook the ashes out of his pipe, re-packed and lit it. It was time to get serious. Karl found a double pinochle and a straight in the hand he was dealt. They won easily and then disposed of three challengers before losing a game.

Karl didn't mind. He suggested they go up on deck and get some fresh air.

Heinrich agreed.

They emerged to a bright sunny deck, where the temperature, balanced between a high sun and an ocean breeze, was just about right. It would have been ideal, except that the small deck allocated to the steerage passengers was jammed with people, and it was aft of a smoke stack which showered the deck with ash. There was standing room only. Young children darted around the crowded deck pursuing each other in a hide-and-seek game. Single young men and women, seg-regated in separate compartments, used the deck to size each other up. Karl and Heinrich moved next to a lifeboat so they had something to lean against.

Heinrich was wondering, "Why, when just about everyone on board is in steerage, do we get this little crowded patch of the deck that is showered with ashes?"

"Remember, you didn't pay for a luxury passage."

"Ya, shouldn't be hard to remember."

"This will all change when we get to America."

"That's right, and how are you going to get rich in America?

Karl revealed his plans to Heinrich. He would go to Omaha, work enough to get a stake, then homestead some land.

Heinrich's plans were more open-ended.

"I will be broke, well, almost broke when I get to Baltimore. That is where I will start, see what comes up."

"Simple plan."

"It's all I can afford."

Two women were sitting on a large coil of rope near where Karl and Heinrich were standing. The older woman was thin, had dark straight hair done in a bun, thin lips, pale skin and wore a perpetual frown. In contrast, the younger of the two had a rosy complexion, blonde hair done in pigtails, and a healthy physique not completely camouflaged by her loose, full-length dress. They both wore shawls around their shoulders to protect them from the cool ocean breeze. Although they appeared to have little in common physically, the way they were conversing and their body language suggested that they were mother and daughter.

Heinrich addressed them. "How do you two rate a place to sit?"

The older woman looked Heinrich over carefully, then replied, "A gentleman gave it up to us."

Heinrich assured her, "A gentleman for sure and there are damn few of us these days. My friend here, Herr Karl Mueller, is one, and I'm Herr Heinrich Schlicter."

The younger woman was smiling by this time, but the older woman maintained her frown. Despite the frown she replied pleasantly enough, "Pleased to meet you. I'm Frau Emily Schumacker and this is my daughter Fraulein Greta Schumacker."

"Are you enjoying the trip?" Heinrich asked.

The two women looked at him strangely. "Enjoy? That is not the word that comes to mind," Frau Schumacker replied. "There are over a hundred women in our compartment, many more than there is room for. No privacy and the ship's crew always nosing around."

"Ship's crew!" Heinrich exclaimed. "We never see any of them in our compartment."

"You're lucky. They always seem to be looking for something."

"Why do they allow that?"

"Who are they? They are them. We just try not to be noticed."

Heinrich tried to be encouraging, "In a few days we will be in Baltimore. Better days are ahead."

"Hope so. My husband is going to meet us in Baltimore. He has been there over a year now."

The daughter, Fraulein Schumacker, had not been saying anything, but scrutinized the two young men carefully. "Will you be staying in Baltimore?" she asked.

"I'll be staying there. Herr Mueller will be heading west, wants to homestead some land," Heinrich replied.

Karl had to go through an explanation of what homesteading meant and where Omaha was.

Fraulein Schumacker thought homesteading in the west sounded interesting. "What is the west like?" she asked.

Karl did not have a ready answer. He had been assured that there was good farming land on the western frontier, and that it could be claimed as one's own. What was it like exactly? He had concepts based largely on his Prussian experience and from anecdotal information he had gotten from people not much more knowledgeable than he was. Karl had to admit that he didn't know what it was really like. "I have heard that there is good farm land to be claimed and that's why I'm going to Omaha. I will find out for sure when I get there."

They visited until the sun dropped low on the horizon and the ocean air began to cool down. The women decided it was time to go below, as much as they dreaded returning to the compartment. Frau Schumacker said they had enjoyed the visit, and she volunteered that she and her daughter came out on the deck every afternoon when the weather was accommodating. "Maybe we will see you again before the voyage ends."

"Very likely, hard to get lost on this little patch of deck," Heinrich replied.

Karl was more affirmative. "We will look for you," he offered.

During the remaining days of the voyage, they did often meet Emily and Greta Schumacker when they were taking in the fresh air on the deck.

As the ship neared its destination, a common sickness swept the ship. Heinrich came down with the sniffles, but got over it in a couple of days. It was not a serious sickness. There was a death in the family compartment, but it was not clear that it was related to the sickness going around. If there had been an outbreak of cholera, scarlet fever, or typhoid, or some other fatal disease, it would soon have been obvious and nothing could have been done about it accept to comfort the sick and dispose of the bodies of those that died. This response to fatal diseases on ships was not that different from the reaction to them on land. There were no effective treatments for any of these diseases, on ships or on land.

The sickness on the ship seemed to have run its course and Karl had hopes that he wouldn't be affected. Karl hardly ever got sick, and when he did it was usually a mild case of whatever it was. However, two days before they were to dock, he was hit hard. His throat became raw, his head was congested, and he developed a hoarse cough.

When the SS *Ohio* moved up Chesapeake Bay, the immigrants knew they were near the end of the voyage. The deck allocated to steerage passengers was continually crowded as immigrants jostled for the opportunity to catch a glimpse of American soil and to catch a whiff of the smells from the nearby shoreline. The land they were seeing and the smells they were inhaling confirmed that they were nearing the end of a very uncomfortable experience.

Before entering the harbor at Baltimore, the ship stopped and a launch came alongside. Karl, despite his illness, was on deck, preferring the fresh air and the unfolding harbor scene to the foul compartment. He and Heinrich leaned on the rail and watched while two people dressed in blue uniforms got off the launch and boarded the ship.

Emily and Greta Schumacker joined Karl and Heinrich.

"Must be American authorities," Heinrich guessed. "What do you think they want?"

Emily Schumacker volunteered that they were checking to see if the ship was carrying the plague, smallpox, something like that.

Karl, still suffering from whatever was afflicting him, hoarsely expressed the hope that they didn't check him. They might quarantine the whole ship.

The Americans looked around the ship, examined some passengers, and departed in less than half an hour. The ship proceeded.

Before docking, the passengers were all sent back to their compartments where members of the crew handed out slates about a foot long and four inches wide with a loop of thin rope attached. The passengers were directed to hang the loop of rope about their neck so the slates hung suspended over their chests.

The slate detail came up to Heinrich. "Name?"

"Heinrich Schlicter."

A man searched the manifest list. "Number 1172."

Another man wrote the number on the slate with chalk.

They did the same thing with Karl.

The ship was tied to a dock twenty feet wide which lay between the ship and a long single-story, gable-roofed structure that looked like a warehouse. The building was twice the length of the ship, and from the pitch of the roof, appeared to be forty to fifty feet wide. Other wharfs with similar buildings protruded into the bay on both sides of where they docked. Half a dozen large grain elevators and a jumble of rail tracks filled the area behind the waterfront.

The immigrants were assembled into groups on the main deck as crewmen shouted numbers in sequences of thirty.

Heinrich looked at his number, 1172, and Karl's 1101. "Looks like we are going to be in different herds. Don't know if I will see you again, so good luck with your homestead."

"When I get rich, I will look you up."

"In that case, I won't expect to see you again."

Karl laughed and waved.

As each group assembled, they moved down the gangplank and into the nearby building. Each group's sea trunks were piled onto a four-wheeled cart that followed the immigrants into the building.

As they moved into the building, Karl's relief at having finished the voyage was being replaced by a feeling of apprehension.

The passengers had talked about the immigration inspection process during the crossing. There would be a physical examination. There would be questions and documents to check. This was the final barrier, the last step in the process, and not everyone would make it through the final gate.

This knowledge now loomed large in Karl's mind. His sickness was still affecting him. That was a concern but Karl was sure it was a common sickness that would soon be over. His real worry was that it might bring attention to him and to another problem that he had become aware of during the last few days.

In France, he had contracted some kind of an infection. The army doctor said it was a venereal infection, not uncommon in the Prussian army, but not serious, not syphilis. A soaking solution had apparently cleared up the problem—at least until now.

Within the last couple of days, Karl had noticed a sore that did not heal, and he did not have the medication that seemed to work before. The sore persisted and became the focus of his concern as he stood in the line waiting to go through immigration.

When Karl's group moved deeper into the building, it was confined to a narrow passageway where two men standing on a raised platform could observe them as they slowly moved through the passageway. Every once in a while one of the men would make a mark on an immigrant's slate as they moved past them. Karl couldn't suppress a croup-like cough as he moved near the observers and one of them made a mark on his slate. As the immigrants came out of the narrow passageway, they entered a large open space where those that had their slates marked were separated from the main group. There were four individuals that had been singled out. One of them, an old, frail, and distraught looking woman, assessed the situation.

"We didn't pass the screen," she said, and then with tears forming in her eyes continued, "I have nothing to go back to."

Karl glanced around and realized that all the people in the group displayed some obvious physical symptom. One man was lame, the other had a vacant look that never went away, the woman was very old and frail, and Karl was displaying the effects of some kind of sickness. The men and the woman in the group were now separated and sent in different directions for physical examinations.

The men entered a room where they were told to remove their shirts. They were lined up and were inspected by two doctors who were assisted by an interpreter. They checked each person as they moved to head of the line. After the inspection some people went one way and others another.

All this was happening so fast that Karl was only reacting. He was not concerned about the sickness, whatever it was, but he was worried about the further scrutinizing it was exposing him to.

The interpreter asked if Karl had any diseases or other medical problems.

"No," Karl answered. "Have some kind of common sickness, got it about three days ago."

His pulse was checked and a stethoscope was applied to his chest and back while the interpreter told him to breath deeply and then to cough. His eyes, ears, and teeth were examined. All of this was of no concern to Karl. He considered himself a generally healthy young man, but when the interpreter told him to drop his pants, his concern grew. The sore was in plain view. How observant was this doctor and what was he looking for? The interpreter told him to squeeze it. Karl did as he was directed. He felt light headed, the room seemed to rotate, and he was not sure he could maintain his balance. The doctor and the interpreter exchanged words in English. Karl imagined a large "rejected" written on his papers and a trip back to Germany.

"All right," the interpreter ordered. "Get your cloths on, go through the door on the right, and you will be directed from there."

In a daze Karl did as he was told.

He entered another room. This one was large, like a meeting hall.

An interpreter standing by the door directed Karl into one of the lines of immigrants being processed.

The immigration official processing the line Karl stood in was looking disheveled by the time Karl reached his post. It was now the middle of the afternoon and processing had been going on all day. The official noted Karl's manifest number and located his form on a table in back of where he worked. He began going through a checklist.

"Karl, Karl Mueller. It's been a long day. Where in Germany did you come from?"

"West Prussia, town of Flatow."

"What kind of work did you do?"

"Farm worker."

"Can you read, write?"

"Ya."

"Know any English?"

"No."

The questioner paused for a moment. "Hum, you went through the medical check. I need to verify something, I will be right back."

Karl now knew the worst was about to happen. The immigration officer would find that Karl had failed the physical inspection. So this is how it would end. It almost didn't matter any longer; Karl was resigned to his fate. The immigration official came back, and continued with a few more questions. After finishing, he made some notes, then handed Karl a piece of paper.

"We are finished, you are accepted to immigrate into the United States. This is your landing card. Good luck."

Karl was stunned. He had so convinced himself that all was lost that he hardly knew how to react.

*"Danke, Danke!"*

He reached out to shake the hand of the interviewer.

*"Danke."*

The interviewer seemed a little surprised at Karl's reaction. "You are welcome. Now you can move along. More are waiting."

Karl got up and moved towards the end of the hall where immigrants holding landing cards were being directed to where foreign currency, notes, gold and other exchangeable valuables could be converted into dollars. Karl got in the line to exchange the thalers he had sewn into his coat. He felt the part of the coat where they were sewn, but felt nothing. Panicking, he felt around the spot where they should be. Nothing. He bent down and examined the place where the thalers should be. The thread used to sew the thalers into the coat had been pulled out. His money was gone. Karl's brief elation at having received a landing card now evaporated. He was stunned. Was he being tested? Was God punishing him—for what? He had checked the coat last night, before he went to sleep. The thalers had been there.

"Move up, the line is moving," someone behind urged.

Karl staggered out of the line. What now?

He assessed his situation. He held a landing card in his hand, he was in America and he had cleared immigration. The only thing that had changed was that he did not have the price of a ticket to Nebraska. That could be remedied, this was the land of opportunity, right? "*Richtig*," he said, answering his own question.

Karl picked up his trunk and walked to the exit and America. He was penniless, he did not know where he would spend the night, and he had a bad sickness. At that moment life seemed good.

# CHAPTER 5

▼

# THE FIRST DAY

Every day since leaving Flatow, Karl had been stressed. He had been living in a state of continuous anxiety as he encountered new challenges on a daily basis. He had anticipated that upon reaching America, upon clearing immigration, his life would begin to normalize. However as he walked out of the immigration facility it was becoming apparent that conditions could become even more stressful. He realized that he could not understand most of what was being said around him. He could not read the signs and notices. He was in a strange land among strange people speaking a strange language.

Karl exited the immigration building into the bright afternoon sunlight and observed his surroundings. Near the wharf where they landed were four other docks and associated warehouses where two other ships were tied up. Other docks and warehouses were visible on the far side of the narrow bay. Half a dozen grain elevators were located a short distance from the waterfront. The elevators and dockside warehouses were served by a complex of railroad tracks that filled most of the space between the buildings. Karl joined the German immigrants terminating their journey in Baltimore. They were milling about, seemingly uncertain about what to do next. Standing among them were Emily and Greta Schumacker.

Karl called to them. "Your husband here?"

"We have not seen him yet. Hope he got the letter telling him what ship we would be on. And you? We thought you would be on the train going west."

"Me too." Karl started telling them his bad experience when they heard some-one else hail them.

It was Heinrich. "Hey, we all meet again. That's good. Karl, what the hell you doing out here? You are supposed to be on the way to Nebraska."

Karl continued his sad story. He concluded, "My money is gone. I'm stuck in Baltimore like you, Heinrich."

"How could that have happened? Do you think it was Paul in the bunk below? You can never trust a Bavarian. He was kind of shifty, I thought."

"I don't know. I always slept on my coat, but this morning it wasn't under my head. I thought I rolled off it. No matter, nothing can be done about it."

"Too bad, but you are right, nothing can be done about it."

"Anyway, I'm in the same boat as you are now. Worse, I don't have any money at all."

"Well, we can share what I have, which is five dollars and a few pennies. That should last a day or two."

"That is damn generous."

"There is a real high rate of interest."

"Somehow that doesn't seem important right now."

"So what do we do now? We can't stay here." Heinrich turned to Emily and Greta. "What are you going to do?"

"Wait for my husband, that is all we can do."

There were a large number of horse drawn wagons arrayed near the immigra-tion building exit. They were fitted to haul passengers and looking for fares.

Heinrich was thinking out loud. "It looks like we are in the middle of nowhere. Wonder what it costs to rent a ride?"

Karl answered, "Ride to where?"

There was a wagon near where Karl stood, a rig and horses that showed a lot of wear. A stout driver with a reddish beard searched the exiting immigrants for a fare.

Karl approached him. Other than immigration officials, he had never spoken to an American before. This driver must speak German, or else how could he solicit German immigrants?

"Can you tell me where there is a place to stay?"

The red-bearded driver looked Karl up and down.

"Do you have the fare?" The driver answered in a German dialect that was dif-ficult for Karl to understand.

"How much is the fare?"

"Fifty cents into town, ten cents each added rider."

Karl had trouble understanding the value of American money, but he knew that for him, any amount was impossible.

"Can you give me directions? Is it far?"

The driver looked at Karl in disgust. "I just take fares, I don't give directions. You Germans are all alike. Don't have money or wouldn't spend it if you had it."

Another driver overheard the exchange and spoke to the driver in German. "Fritz, you are a German."

"Was German. I fought with the union. Citizen now."

"Once a German, always a German. It don't wash off."

"So, I should know they are a bunch of tightwads."

This exchange was enough to discourage Karl from inquiring further, and a look at the other drivers reinforced his decision. Heinrich had listened to the exchange and lifted his sea trunk on his shoulder. "We need to get away from this place. Won't find a place standing here."

Karl agreed. "Looks like some bigger buildings over there." Karl pointed up the bay. "Probably the middle of Baltimore. Can't be more than a few kilometers."

He turned to Emily and Greta. "You sure you want to wait here?"

"We have to wait."

"Good luck then."

The women watched wistfully as Karl and Heinrich shouldered their trunks and started down the wagon-road that headed towards the main part of the town.

The road Karl and Heinrich were following crossed the numerous railroad tracks near the docks and entered an area that was a mix of dilapidated warehouses, workshops and small factories. As they proceeded further, the road turned into a street, and structures housing people were added to the mix. Karl was taken aback at the conditions in which the people were living. They houses hardly looked habitable and could be best described as hovels. Most of them looked like they had been made from scrape wood and weren't any bigger than a good-sized room. The people visible around these structures and the people on the street were Negroes. Karl had never seen Negroes before and found himself studying them closely, as if they were some exotic creatures. The street they were walking on was unpaved, dry, and dusty. Accumulated animal waste and garbage lay about attracting hordes of flies. If the streets in America were paved with gold, this one apparently had been missed.

Finally, Karl voiced some of his thoughts. "I hope this isn't how all Americans live. Animals do better in Prussia."

Heinrich shifted his trunk to the other shoulder. "Ya, for sure. Do you think Negroes are still slaves? They seem to be free to come and go."

"You know, this is funny in a way. Everything we own is on our shoulders, we haven't eaten all day, we don't know where we will sleep tonight, and we are worried about these poor devils. They probably have a roof of some kind, a place to sleep, something to eat."

Heinrich had to agree with that. "Seeing this makes me wonder about some of the stories we heard. Everyone in America is supposed to be rich or getting rich. Looks like a few got left out, and we aren't off to a very good start."

As they moved on, conditions did not improve, but the neighborhood became all residential. There were still some makeshift shacks, but most of the buildings were more substantial, though just as run down. The people were changing too. There were still Negroes, however most of the people were white like Heinrich and Karl, although they didn't look any more prosperous than the Negroes. The dirt streets were filled with garbage, noise, many children darting about, laundry hanging out of windows, older youths, and some adults lounging on building steps.

Karl was becoming more concerned. He had expected things would be different, but had not anticipated the ugliness and squalor that he was now observing. He was relieved when they started seeing improvements in the neighborhood they were moving through. The streets became cleaner and were covered with paving stones. Brick row houses with marble front steps lined these streets. A short time after reaching this better neighborhood they come upon a market. There were stores, a butcher shop, a bakery, and vendor carts in the street. Karl was reminded that he had not eaten since leaving the ship, but he did not have a penny in his pocket, and wasn't going to bring up the subject of eating. Besides, the first priority was to find some place to stay, after which they would know how much money they had for food, if any.

Karl stopped in front of a fruit vendor's cart and asked, "*Sprechen Sie Deutsch?*" There was a turning of the head from side to side. They stopped at another vendor selling loaves of bread. Same result. Heinrich pointed to the butcher shop which had a recognizable name in the window: Schade's. "That looks like a German name."

They entered the small shop. Sausages of various kinds hung in the window. Two small display cases were filled with fresh meat and more sausages. A massive chopping block sat between the two display cases. A portly middle-aged man with an untrimmed mustache and wearing a soiled, blood-stained apron stood behind one of the display cases.

Karl's inquiry drew a response in perfect German.

*Kann ich ihnen helfen?* Are you lost? Just get here?

The sea trunks they were carrying answered the last question which Karl confirmed. "Ya, just arrived." He pointed to Heinrich. "Herr Heinrich Schlicter. I'm Herr Karl Mueller."

The man held out his hand, Herr Paul Schade.

Karl continued, "Do you know where we could find a place to stay? Someplace that don't cost too much."

"You want to sleep cheap? Ya. I know how that goes, got here five years ago. There are places, not too far from here. Maybe don't smell so good, not pretty, but cheap."

Karl affirmed that it had to be cheap. He had been thirsty for some time and he asked Paul if they could have some water.

"Sure," Paul answered, pointing to a pail with a dipper sitting on a table behind a display case. "Help yourself."

Karl and Heinrich drank their fill.

"How have things been for you in America?" Karl asked.

"The first couple of years were hard, better since. Getting by. What part of Germany are you from?"

When Karl mentioned Flatow, Prussia, Paul exclaimed, "My family is from Wollmitz, a little village east of Flatow!"

"I know it well," Karl replied.

"Someone from Flatow needs more than water to drink." He reached into his cupboard and came up with three bottles of beer. "You must be hungry. I'll fix you a sausage sandwich."

Karl protested, "That would be too much."

Heinrich quickly overrode Karl's protestations. "That would be much appreciated." Paul rummaged through a cupboard and came out with a summer sausage, real German dark bread, some large sweet onions, and mustard. He cut slices of sausage and sweet onions, spread mustard over the bread, piled on the sausage and onions, and handed sandwiches to the two hungry men.

They talked about the old country, and the new one.

A customer came in. After Paul waited on him, they continued to talk.

Heinrich wanted to know if there were many Germans in Baltimore.

"Lots of German immigrants, Irish, some Italians lately. What are you fellows planning to do?"

Karl described his plans "For now, earn enough money to get to Nebraska."

Paul had never heard of Nebraska.

Some more talk and it was time for Karl and Heinrich to move on and find lodging for the night.

Paul gave them directions. "You just look for 'For Rent' signs." He showed them what the words "For Rent" looked like.

Karl realized from the directions that they would be backtracking to the neighborhood that he was critical of when they passed through it earlier that afternoon. He commented, "We came through there earlier."

"If you want cheap, that is where it is, between here and nigger town."

They returned to the garbage-littered streets that they had passed through earlier in the day and soon found a building with a "For Rent" sign on it. It was located on a street of almost identical two-story wood frame buildings set side by side for the full length of the block. The building featured unwashed window panes, some cracked and in some cases replaced with paper or cardboard.

There was a small sign in English on the door.

Karl looked at the sign. "What you think it says?"

"Don't know. Try knocking."

Knocking did not seem to work. Karl tried the door, and it opened into a dim hallway littered with debris and garbage. They could hear a baby crying in one of the rooms. Hesitantly, they stepped in. A smell of stale clothes and unwashed bodies enveloped them as they moved into the building. There was another door to their left, with another sign on it, again a puzzle to the two Germans.

Karl knocked.

The door opened, and a small, gaunt man with a sallow complexion and bloodshot eyes surveyed the two young men. He noted the sea trunks the men were carrying.

"Just off the boat?" he asked in English. He held out a hand, "Andrew is my name."

Karl and Heinrich looked at each other. Language was going to be a problem.

The landlord must have come to the same conclusion. He started talking in English, as if to no one in particular. "I have a couple of rooms open, prefer to deal only with Americans, but will consider anyone except niggers and single women. Follow me, I'll show you the room."

He started off, and Karl and Heinrich followed.

As they walked, the proprietor continued to talk, muttering to himself. "Foreigners, just off the boat, probably have little or no money."

Andrew began the tour by showing them a washroom. A set of tubs surrounded by unwashed laundry sat on a low bench. Two metal buckets completed the list of accessories in the wash room. There was a small stove for heating water in the corner of the room, and firewood strewn about and a bucket of coal.

Andrew continued the one-sided conversation, "This is where you wash clothes, take baths if you have a mind to. Get water from the pump at the corner down the street. Empty the water in the alley."

There were two floors. A littered hallway six feet wide ran through the center of the building. A stairway half the width of the hallway led up to the second level. Half the lower level was taken up by the wash room and the landlord's quarters. Two apartments filled the rest of the lower level.

Andrew led them up the stairs. He showed them a room, one of four on the upper level and apparently for rent. It was in back with a window looking out on the alley and a shed that was the privy. The room was ten feet wide and fourteen feet long. Crammed into the space was a double bed, a small table, one chair, a wash stand, a small cupboard with some dishes and tableware, and a small stove that furnished heat and could be used for cooking. An oil lamp sitting on the table furnished light.

The proprietor kept talking as he showed Karl and Heinrich the building and room.

"Don't allow more than four people in a room. Rent due in advance, one week's rent minimum, with an extra week's rent paid before moving in. That is two weeks rent for anyone new. The two of you could share a room for fifteen cents a day each. Buy your own firewood or coal, oil for the lamp."

Karl looked at Heinrich. "Understand anything he is babbling about?"

"Nothing."

The proprietor must have realized as much. When they got back to his office, he started putting numbers on paper, making up a short calendar. With the help of gesturing, and a few words in German that the proprietor knew, he was able to communicate the stark reality of the terms.

Two weeks rent in advance. That was impossible. Heinrich had only five dollars sewn into his jacket.

"Come on, Karl," Heinrich said while picking up his trunk. "We will have to keep looking. Anyway, this place smells bad."

Karl prepared to follow Heinrich.

As they started out the door, the proprietor pulled on Heinrich's sleeve and started talking fast. "We can work this out. It's the amount down, isn't it?"

He started putting more numbers on the paper. Fifteen cents a night each and one week rent in advance.

Karl and Heinrich looked at the numbers again. It was an improved offer, feasible, but it would still consume almost half of their assets.

"It may be the best we can do," Heinrich suggested.

"Ya, and it's getting late."

They shook hands on the deal.

The proprietor pointed to himself and said, "Andrew."

Karl said the word "Andrew" and, pointing to himself. "Karl," then pointing at Heinrich, "Heinrich."

They all laughed and shook hands again.

Karl and Heinrich moved in, which consisted of finding a place for their sea trunks in the crowded room. It had been a long day and they were ready to get some rest.

# CHAPTER 6

▼

# THERE IS WORK FOR EVERYONE

They were up early the next morning. They needed to find work and quickly. Nearly half the money they were sharing was already gone.

It was a grey morning when they left the boardinghouse. People were moving along the street headed for jobs or at least somewhere definite. All except the two immigrants emerging from the rooming house. Karl had no idea where they were going, and he knew that Heinrich didn't either. But Karl was feeling upbeat. He was off the ship, he had made it through immigration, his cold was getting better, and he felt optimistic about finding work. He had been told there was work for everyone in America and he had no reason to doubt that. He had another sensation—he was hungry.

"Heinrich, I'm starving."

"I'm agreeing with that. We have to invest in something to eat."

"What are we down to?"

"We still have two dollars and ninety cents. I think I see a bakery. We should be able to afford a loaf of bread."

Through the use of sign language and numbers on paper, they found a loaf of bread could be bought for ten cents. That would be breakfast.

Now to begin the job search. They started walking down a street, sharing the loaf of bread that they had just bought. They walked towards the mass of large buildings that would be the center of the city. They found the streets in the city's center filled with offices, stores, and saloons.

Heinrich observed, "This doesn't look like a strong back kind of street."

"Ya, talking, reading and writing in English isn't what we do."

They headed towards the docks. Their kind of work might be more plentiful in that direction.

Heinrich was wondering, "How do we know who to talk to?"

"In German?"

"Ya, in German, that could be a problem."

They stopped near where a crew was loading cargo onto a ship.

There was a man who was standing mostly, watching, occasionally speaking in a way that sounded like an order.

Karl screwed up his courage and approached the man. He held out his hands and said one of the few words of English that he knew. "Work?"

Karl understood the man's answer: "No."

They tried a couple of other places.

Looking for a job was a new experience for Karl. Growing up in a small community in West Prussia did not prepare him for this kind of thing. In Prussia, if you didn't go into a trade or if your family didn't have a business, you would work on the Hohenzollern estate. It was a simple, uncomplicated and anxiety-free system. It was not anything like the situation the two young immigrants faced as they wandered along the streets of Baltimore. It occurred to Karl that the two of them didn't know how to go about looking for a job.

Karl shared his concerns with Heinrich, "We can't just walk around. We could be walking past jobs, or looking in the wrong places."

"So, what should we do?"

"I don't know, maybe find somebody German that we can talk to, somebody who knows something about how to find a job."

"Where is this German? Paul the butcher said there were a lot of them around."

"How about one of those saloons we went by?"

The idea appealed to Heinrich. "And get a beer. What does a beer cost? I think I saw something on the window, maybe three cents, five cents. We could afford a beer, one beer, for five cents or less."

"First we find out if they can help us, then we buy a beer."

"For sure."

They backtracked to one of the places they had passed, found it open, and entered into a darkened interior. It was noon and there were a large number of patrons taking their lunch. The clients were a mixture of businessmen, office workers and tradesmen. The haze and smell of cigar smoke mixed with the odor of stale beer hung heavy, tempered to a degree by the aroma of food from a table in the middle of the room. There was a hum of male voices. A long bar ran along one side, tables and chairs along the other, and in the middle stood a long table covered with bread, vegetables, cheese, sausage, ribs, and pickles. Behind the bar were bottles of whiskey, wine, and rum. A tapped beer keg was ready to fill stacked mugs.

A man in a white apron behind the bar was serving the noon rush. A Negro kept the food table stocked from a source in the back of the establishment and picked up after the customers. Another man stood at the end of the bar at the change drawer, keeping close tabs on what was going on while he made change.

Karl and Heinrich stood near the entrance for quite a long time, just observing. The man at the change drawer looked over at them occasionally. Karl began to feel uneasy, a little intimidated.

"Do you see someone to talk to?"

"I see a lot of people."

"Ya. How about the bartender?"

"He's busy." Several men stood at the bar."What the hell, I'll ask one of those men at the bar."

The men shook their heads and put up their hands, indicating they didn't comprehend.

A man sitting at one of the side tables, working on a beer and a stack of ribs, motioned to them. He was dressed as a proprietor or office worker, in a coat and starched collar. He was a smallish man with a rotund body, a round face, and a neatly trimmed Van Dyke beard.

He stood up, walked over to the two men, and extended a hand towards Karl and Heinrich. "*Wie geht's*? Herr Emil Schmels, can I be of assistance?" He spoke a German dialect different than Karl and Heinrich were accustomed to, but it was understandable.

Karl was relieved to hear the guttural sounds. "We could use help. Just got here, trying to find our way around."

"Looking for work?"

"Ya, that's for sure."

"Want to get something to drink, eat? We can talk about it. You could buy a beer for five cents, but if you pay ten cents, you get a beer and as much as you want to eat from the table over there. If you prefer whiskey, add ten more cents."

Karl and Heinrich exchanged glances.

It was a little expensive for their budget, but they did need to eat, and if they could get some useful information, it would be worth it.

"What do you think," Heinrich asked, "Should we have a ten-cent beer?"

"Ya, and something to eat."

"Go ahead," Emil encouraged. "Load up and we can talk."

The men followed his advice, bought beer, and loaded up on sausages, ribs, green onions, bread, and radishes for starters.

They then discussed the job prospects in Baltimore. "You should have been here a couple of years ago," explained Emil. "Jobs were looking for workers. But now things are not so good. Things have slowed down. You really have to know where the jobs are, and how to get them. Good jobs. Some jobs, you will work your ass off and barely make enough to eat and pay for a place to sleep. That's no good, that's not what you came across the ocean to do."

As Emil talked, Karl grew concerned. What he was hearing was not encouraging. Unlimited opportunities for anyone who had the ambition to take them on were what he expected. Limited opportunities was what he was now hearing. Karl was beginning to realize that many of his fantasies about America might be just that.

Emil continued explaining the prospects for finding work and the way to approach the problem. The advantage of having assistance in finding those opportunities was what Emil was describing. He revealed that he was actually in the business of helping people like Karl and Heinrich.

Emil explained, "Using a knowledgeable person to aid in your job search makes sense. You will know what opportunities there are. There is a small fee but it's worth the cost many times over."

What Emil was saying did make sense. "How does it work?"

"Well," Emil explained, "There is a small retainer fee you pay, and you are given information about jobs available. I assist in applying for the job, act as an interpreter, explain the terms of the employment to you. If and when you accept a job as a result of this assistance, you make a final service payment. There is a one dollar retainer and a dollar owed after the job is accepted and that dollar owed wouldn't have to be paid until you get your first pay. I can have a list of jobs lined up by noon tomorrow if you want to go ahead."

Karl and Heinrich were silent for a while after Emil finished his offer.

Heinrich asked, "A dollar each?"

"Ya, a dollar each."

Heinrich looked at Karl. "We need to talk about this."

Emil agreed. "I got to take a leak. When I get back, if you need more time, let me know."

After Emil had left, Heinrich turned to Karl. "I think you know that we would have only sixty cents left if we do this."

"That is about what I figured. It's up to you, your money. Maybe we could get the retainer reduced."

Emil would not bend on the retainer, and finally Heinrich accepted the original proposal.

Heinrich dug out the money, handed it to Emil and asked, "All right Emil, when do we get the job list?"

"Here at noon tomorrow," was the reply. Emil dug out a piece of paper and scribbled a receipt, signed and dated it. They shook hands on the deal, and Karl and Heinrich then made their way out to the street.

Karl was relieved that the job search puzzle was being solved. They spent the rest of the afternoon sightseeing and loafing and were ready to rest when they got back to the rooming house.

The next morning they slept in. When they finally got up they were famished. Heinrich suggested going back to the bakery and getting a loaf of bread again. Once at the bakery, it was hard to resist some grape jam to go with the bread and tea to wash it down. Twenty cents.

"With a job we should be able to get credit for a few days, be able to eat until pay day," Heinrich reasoned.

They arrived at the saloon at noon and surveyed the clientele. Emil had not arrived. It was difficult waiting. They were down to forty cents and they weren't ready to spend any of it until they took a look Emil's list of jobs.

Time passed slowly. Karl was becoming uneasy. "Where is that Emil? He said he would be here at noon. That is twelve o'clock where I come from. It's almost one."

Karl became aware that the owner was watching them. The lunch rush was winding down and the proprietor was approaching them. He was speaking in English,

"No loitering in here. Get." Then, sensing that they were Germans, he threw in some German words that he knew, "*Roust, roust mit du.*"

He was a big man and pushed the two surprised men toward the door.

They didn't resist and after the door closed behind them, Karl suddenly realized what had happened. They had been conned, duped out of most of the money they had left.

"That son of a bitch took us."

What had occurred then dawned on Heinrich. "I'll kill the fat little bastard," he hissed.

Karl agreed, "I'd like to kill the little worm, if we could find him, but it might cause more problems than it would be worth. We aren't very far from the immigration depot. They could have us on a boat heading back before we knew what happened."

"The way things are going, that might not be all bad."

What it boiled down to was that they had forty cents between them, no jobs, and the rent would be due in four more days.

Karl looked down the street. "Let's get going, see how many no's we can collect before it gets dark."

They got quite a few no's and more the next day. People weren't hiring, and if they were it would probably be somebody they could talk to.

Thoughts of food were becoming an obsession. Their daily diet was now a shared loaf of bread washed down with water. Heinrich remembered Paul the butcher. "Maybe he has some sausage and beer left."

"That would be sort of like begging."

"Ya."

"And that won't help pay the rent. We could be on the street in a couple of days."

Friday morning they spent the last dime on a loaf of bread. They were not getting enough to eat, which put even more strain on the task of looking for work. Karl and Heinrich had not been carrying any extra weight before starting this unwanted fast, and their clothes were hanging looser each day. The twinkle in Heinrich's eyes dimmed and his enthusiasm flagged. Karl was feeling the strain. Comparing their experiences with a peasant's fate did not come out well. Peasants had work. If nothing else they had more than enough work. And usually enough to eat. It might only be potatoes, but there was always something. Peasants might live in a small drafty cottage, but it wasn't surrounded by the filth of others.

When they arrived at the rooming house Friday evening after a futile day of looking for work, Andrew met them at the door. Karl and Heinrich did not have to know English to know what he wanted.

Andrew soon realized that his roomers had not found work and had no money. It was about as clear a case for eviction as there could be.

Karl was surprised at the landlord's reaction. Andrew made indications that they should wait. He went off and was soon back with someone in tow.

The person Andrew brought with him addressed them in German. He introduced himself as Herr Johann Wellman who lived on the first level with his wife and two small children. "Hear you are having a little problem getting situated."

Heinrich corrected him. "Big problem."

"Well, Andrew is willing to help you out on the rent side, and I can help one of you with a job, if you don't mind doing nigger work."

"Nigger work?" Karl questioned.

"Work nobody wants to do. Since the war, niggers do it mostly. Anyway, I work in a saloon, tend bar, and we need someone to clean, wash dishes, stock the buffet, tap kegs. Keep you busy, ten to ten, six days a week, fifty cents a day plus food. Get paid at the end of each day."

As desperate for work as Karl was, he was hesitant. "Sounds like a couple of notches below peasant work."

Heinrich was not so critical. "Plus food, I'll do it."

"Can you start tomorrow?"

"Why not? Sure I can."

Andrew, watching the conversation, showed visible relief when Johann told him that they had an understanding. Heinrich would start working tomorrow and would be paid at the end of the day.

"Tell them they can pay day-to-day until they get caught up. That means they can pay me thirty cents for tomorrow and they will be current with the rent."

Satisfied that the emergency was over, Andrew left. Johann stayed on to talk some more.

"That bastard isn't doing you a favor. He would have two rooms empty if he turned you out. He knew I was looking for help and he kept one of his rooms filled."

Karl wasn't going to complain about their good fortune. "Whatever the reason, *danke* Herr Wellman. Is there any chance you would know about any other jobs?

"Lucky for Heinrich I knew about that job. There aren't many around."

Heinrich was paying the rent and smuggling food for Karl from the saloon. It took a lot of the pressure off, but Karl still needed a job. During a day of job hunting, Karl found himself in the market area where Paul's butcher shop was located. Karl thought, "Why not stop and visit with Paul?"

Paul remembered Karl and Heinrich. He was sorry they were having trouble finding work.

"Do you know anything about butchering?" Paul asked.

"My oldest brother is a master butcher in Prussia. I have worked with him. We butchered at home."

"Not that it matters. "Paul continued, "I get my fresh meat from a wholesale butcher, quarters, and halves. Two German master butchers do the slaughtering. Heard they were looking for a helper. I'll see what I can find out. Stop by in a day or two."

Karl stopped by the next day and the day after that. On the third day Paul said the master butchers wanted to talk to him.

The butchers described the job for what it was, "A shitty job, cleaning up, do the dirty work so we can keep cutting meat. Seventy-five cents a day, six days a week, usually twelve hours, sometimes less. Start right away."

Karl took the job.

# CHAPTER 7

▼

# SETTLING IN

Having found work and a place to live, Karl and Heinrich settled in. The anxiety that had been part of their lives since arriving in America subsided. Karl's cold had long since gone away and the sore that had concerned him at the immigration screening had healed itself. They were not living high, but considering where they had been, things had improved.

Karl assessed his situation. He was making seventy-five cents a day, six days a week. That was four dollars and fifty cents a week. Food wouldn't cost him much. Karl and the master butchers would throw some fresh meat on a fire pit they had at work, which, along with some bread, made a decent noon meal. He would carry some meat home, fry it up, and have it with some boiled or fried potatoes for supper. He did have to buy the potatoes, tea, coffee, other incidentals. He figured this would cost a dollar a week. Lodging was a dollar and five cents a week. Realistically, he knew he was going to spend another dollar a week on things like tobacco, clothes, and an occasional beer. He had found out the fare to Omaha was ten dollars. He was not going to leave without having a little cushion. He wanted to avoid the kind of anxiety he faced when arriving in America. So what it boiled down to was that he would have to spend about half a year building up the fund for his ticket, traveling money, and a cushion.

The job suited Karl. German was the language used. He got along well with the two master butchers, finding them easy to work with. Kermit was a large powerful man who used his strength to overpower obstacles. Pete was the opposite in many ways. Smaller in size, he made every move count, using leverage when he could. Using technique rather than muscle, he was able to hold up his end. The two men knew their business. Kermit talked a lot, when he was working and when he wasn't. Pete listened mostly, but could hold his own if the subject interested him.

Time passed quickly for the two men who were working six twelve hour days a week. The uncomfortable sticky Baltimore summer was giving way to more pleasant fall temperatures when Karl began feeling a vague uneasiness. Sunday was the one day they had to rest and relax and it was something Karl relished, even in the dilapidated rooming house with the sounds of crying babies and neighbors fighting. He used the day as intended, to rest his body and to get it ready for the next week of hard work and long hours. When relaxing, his mind would inevitably bring up images of the past. His thoughts would return to his youth, his family, and Flatow. At times, the realization that he likely would never see his family, home or the Prussian country side weighed heavily on him. There seemed to be a yearning for the familiar, for a connection to the past. One thing that had been part of his youth was attending church on Sundays. If he could find a church, a Lutheran church, an Evangelical Lutheran church, it could provide such a connection to the past.

He mentioned the idea of going to church to Heinrich.

"Why?"

"I always attended church at home. It feels like something is missing."

"I was baptized and confirmed a Lutheran but don't feel a thing."

"Do you think there are any Lutheran churches around?"

"There are a lot of churches, don't know what kind they are. Paul said there were a lot of Germans around. There must be Lutheran churches. One follows the other."

Karl decided he would spend his Sunday afternoon exploring the neighborhood for churches. Heinrich declined the invitation to join in the search. He needed to get rested for the coming week.

There was no shortage of churches in Baltimore. Karl had noticed many in a casual way but had not identified them by type. Now he was looking for a specific type of church, a Lutheran church, and ideally, a German Evangelical Lutheran church. The Catholic churches were easy to identify by their markings and statuary and because they were usually the biggest churches around. The other churches were a little harder to sort out. Karl found a church near the market where Paul's butcher shop was located. Saint Martin's. It was Lutheran and the postings were in German. It had an appealing appearance, brick with stained glass windows and was good-sized. Not as large or impressive as the church his family attended in Flatow, but nice. According to the postings, there was a service in German at eleven a.m.

While Karl made plans to attend services at Saint Martin's the following Sunday, two concerns came to mind. One was that they passed the plate. He would have to put at least a few pennies into the collection plate. Money that he had not planned on spending. The other was that he did not have any going-to-church clothes. Karl had three sets of clothes. Two of these he wore alternately to work. He would wash the set that became filthy with blood and animal waste each night, and wear the alternate set of work clothes the next day. His third set of clothes was a backup that could be substituted for his work clothes. In Prussia everyone had work clothes and a separate set of clothes for going to church. He did not have a go-to-church set of clothes.

Karl made the difficult decision to update his wardrobe. He bought a second hand white shirt and suit coat, a made-up tie, and a starched collar. The best pair of work pants he had would have to do. He trimmed his hair and beard and took a bath.

Heinrich took note. "I'm impressed."

"Better be. Cost me two months savings."

"The Lord will be pleased, I'm sure."

The following Sunday, Karl entered the church and sat in a pew at the back of the church. By the time the service started, the church was filled to capacity. The organ played a familiar prelude and the German looking congregation mentally transported Karl back to his homeland. This was further reinforced as the order of the service followed a known pattern and the organ played familiar hymns. Karl felt pangs of nostalgia as he recited the doxology and sang the hymns. The minister was tall and thin, almost to the point of being gaunt, but he spoke in a strong, authoritative voice. Erect in posture, certain in his pronouncements, he was reminiscent of Lutheran ministers Karl had known in Prussia.

Included among the announcements of church activities was one of an English class for church members that had started the previous week, and was still open to members interested in attending. The class was held in the church every Sunday evening from six to eight o'clock. That peaked Karl's interest. Karl had little opportunity to learn English. German was the only language used where he worked, and Karl and Heinrich always conversed in German.

Partway through the sermon Karl noticed a young woman who seemed familiar seated two rows ahead of him. Suddenly Karl realized that it was Greta Schumacker, the younger of the pair of women that he and Heinrich had made friends with on the ship.

When the service ended, Karl intercepted Greta and greeted her. She was surprised, and seemed a little reticent in responding to his greetings.

"Herr Mueller, what a surprise."

"Ya Fraulein Schumaker, good to see you. How have you been?

"Getting by, and you?"

"Also getting by."

Karl did notice a change in Greta. When he last saw her, the day they got off the ship, despite the rigors of the voyage, she seemed to be radiating a glow that is associated with a young woman. The glow was no longer evident. She did not look Karl in the eye the way she used to. Something had changed.

"Are you alone? Where is your mother?"

A shadow moved across Greta's face. "We never found my father."

Karl did not know what to say. Greta broke the awkward silence.

"We are getting by. My mother takes care of the children for a widower, and I work in the store he runs."

"That is good."

"Ya, that is good."

"Could I walk you to where you live?"

She hesitated, then finally answered, "Maybe some other time."

Karl did not press the subject, but changed it. "The church has a class in English. Did you hear them announce that?"

"Were you thinking of going?"

"I could use it. I have almost no chance to learn English."

"We could all use it."

"Want to go to the class with me?"

"I don't know if I can. I have to talk to Herman."

"Herman?"

"He is the widower we live with."

Karl began to sense the cause of the tentativeness noticed in Greta's behavior. He asked, "You need his permission?"

"We live in his house."

"I plan to be here tonight. Hope you can make it."

They parted, and Karl returned to the rooming house where he found Heinrich still in bed. Considering that he worked until ten o'clock the night before, and then didn't come directly back to the rooming house, that was not unexpected. Karl described his meeting with Greta to Heinrich. "They didn't find her father. They have some arrangement, living with a widower. She did not seem the same, acted a little funny."

"Mm," was Heinrich's reaction. "Weird, meeting Greta like that."

Karl mentioned the English lessons and asked if Heinrich was interested. Heinrich was picking up a fair amount of English at his job in the saloon so didn't feel the same need for the class that Karl had, and declined the invitation.

Greta was at the church when Karl got there.

"Any problem getting permission?" Karl asked.

"No. I told him I would be more help at the store if I knew English. He thought it was a good idea, encouraged me to go."

"It is true."

"A little bit."

Though starting a week late, they were welcomed into the group. There were ten other fledgling English speakers in the group and plenty of room for two more. The English classes were conducted by the church's minister, the same one who had conducted the service earlier in the day. His name was Reverend Paul Wesler. It was soon obvious that Reverend Wesler considered English inferior to high German. English was imprecise, its usage kept changing, the same words could mean completely different things. Despite all of these disadvantages, Reverend Wesler made it clear that he considered it important that his parishioners learn English. They needed to know English if they hoped to succeed in this new country. The curriculum recognized the limitations of a class meeting once a week, attended by individuals on their only day off from working twelve-hour days. The goals were appropriately modest. These were to provide the students with an ability to converse at a fundamental level, and to read enough to recognize signs and the names of things.

It was dark when the class finished, and Greta agreed that Karl could walk her partway home.

While walking, Greta revealed some of the details of the living arrangement she and her mother had with the widower. The widower Hermann Schulze had two children, ages two and six, who had been left motherless when their mother and two other children died of diphtheria last spring.

Greta asked Karl if he remembered the wagon drivers outside the immigration depot last spring. "One of the wagon drivers knew Herman, and when he saw my mother and me stranded, he saw a solution to both Herman's and our problems."

Herman ran a green grocery and Greta and her mother now lived with him and his two children. Five people in two rooms over the green grocery store.

Greta summed up the arrangement. "It did not start out well and has gotten worse. It is hard to talk about."

Karl could now understand the change that he noticed in Greta. He felt a real concern for her situation, but living on the edge as he was, could offer only sympathy.

When they got about a block from the green grocery store where she lived, Greta told Karl she would go the rest of the way by herself. "Herman doesn't like men hanging around."

Karl did not always make church, but when he did, he would find Greta there. She said it was one of the only chances she had of getting away from Herman's watchful eye. Her mother did not even have that opportunity. Herman did not let her mother go anywhere, ever.

Although Karl was finding that learning English was difficult, he never missed a class. Reverend Wesler had described the language as fundamentally flawed, but Karl's difficulties with the language were more personal. He was in his early twenties and the German language had been deeply engraved into his brain and his tonal muscles. German would always be his first language, but he persisted, knowing that if he was going to work his way out of the bottom of the American barrel, one of the requirements was to be conversant in English.

Greta never missed a session either, and after the class, Karl would always walk her to the corner of the block where she lived over the green grocery store. It took about half an hour to walk from the church to where they parted. It was during those walks that they became more at ease in each other's company.

Greta's troubled circumstances and simple garments could not completely hide the comely young woman that she was. It didn't change the golden blonde hair done in a bun, or alternately two long pigtails, or the blue eyes that lit up when she smiled. The simple, full-length dress revealed little, but did not totally fully camouflage her fully developed female form. Karl was not oblivious to these attractions.

During the first few weeks a palpable tension existed as they walked close together but not touching. They made small talk as they walked home from the classes. As familiarity overcame some of their awkwardness, they became more relaxed and more open with each other.

The details of Greta's circumstances became clearer. She and her mother were being treated much like indentured servants by Herman. Besides taking care of Herman's children, they also took care of the green grocery store. Greta's mother had experience running a green grocery store in Germany, so probably knew as much about the business as Herman. Other than watching the women like a hawk when he was around, he didn't do much of anything else. He did spend a lot of time at a local saloon playing cards.

There was one thing Greta had a hard time talking about. Herman made her mother sleep with him.

As troubled as Greta was, as bitter as she seemed at times and as vulnerable as she seemed at other times, a fresh and self-assured pleasant person would often emerge. As Karl learned more about Greta's situation, he was able to better understand her behavior and made allowances for it. In fact, Karl found he was strongly attracted to this elusive person being buffeted by troubling circumstances.

One cold winter evening they pushed against the wind in their walk back to the store. The cold damp air blew through their clothing. Karl put his arm around Greta's waist and pulled her close as a way to help keep her warm. Greta leaned into him, enhancing the closeness and Karl savored the feeling of their bodies pressing together. Normally Karl would walk Greta back to the corner at the end of her block, then leave her there. That evening he insisted on walking her to the store, where they lingered in the cold doorway, holding each other closely. She let her head fall onto his chest. He savored a faint scent in her hair and touched it with his lips. Then bending, touched his lips to her cheek. Greta turned her head slightly and their lips met. Karl had kissed a woman, for the first time in his life.

Karl had never had a close relationship with a woman, only crushes. There was a girl in the Flatow church, the daughter of an aristocrat whose family sat in a private cubical that he used to fantasize about. More realistically there was the daughter of the peasant Ulrich family, Emma, who would smile and drop her eyes whenever they met entering or leaving church. But he had never worked up enough nerve to talk to her, nor had she devised an excuse to start a conversation with Karl.

Not that Karl was a virgin. While he was in the army, visiting French brothels was a form of group recreation, and abstinence hardly seemed to be an option. What Karl had not experienced was the full development of a relationship with a woman, with all of its warmth and complications.

After that first show of affection in the cold store entry, the two did not seem able to leave each other alone. Whenever they were together, they were always touching in some way. They would hold hands and lean on each other in class, and Greta would be on Karl's arm when walking home.

Thoughts of Greta filled Karl's mind constantly and he began looking forward to Sundays with great anticipation.

Kermit noted the distraction. "Karl, sometimes I would swear your mind is lost somewhere. Bet you got a lady friend. That will do it."

Pete joined in, "That could be it, a man with a woman on his mind is just about worthless, unless he's a butcher's helper, then it don't make much difference."

"Ya," Kermit agreed. "Lucky thing."

Karl went along with their joshing speculations, while not acknowledging how close they were to figuring out his situation.

The half-hour walk in the cold dampness of the Baltimore winter and the two hours in the English class offered little opportunity for the greater intimacy the young couple both craved. They found some relief in a small restaurant located on the route from the church. It was a walk-down, family-run Italian restaurant. One could look into the restaurant through sidewalk-level windows and enter by going down six steps. It was small, with only five tables and a counter. Karl and Greta would order two cups of thick black coffee for two cents a cup. They would cut the coffee with cream from a pitcher, then occupy one of the tables until closing time. There were usually no other customers in the restaurant at that time of the day. The only activity was that of Antonio, the father of the family, cleaning up and closing things down.

There they talked, using the time to learn about one another and speculate about the future.

Karl talked about his goal of homesteading land on the western frontier. First he had to save enough money to get to Omaha, Nebraska, then he would have to work to save enough to buy the stock and tools needed to work the homestead.

Greta was looking for an escape, but her options were limited because she was a woman and because she did not want to abandon her mother.

They began to talk about combining their goals. It was complicated because the goals were not compatible. There would have to be compromise. Karl could abandon his plan to go west and hope to improve his situation in Baltimore. Greta could abandon her mother and go west with Karl. There was no resolution to the dilemma as the end of winter approached.

Karl had exceeded the time he had planned to spend in Baltimore. It had taken longer than he planned to save enough money to make the journey to Omaha, but he now had more than the amount necessary.

Heinrich was beginning to wonder about Karl's plans. "You must have enough saved for a ticket by now? The English class holding you up?".

"Can't get too much English," Karl assured him.

"Or is it Greta you can't get too much of?"

"It won't be long now."

Financially Karl was ready to make a move. He could pick up his sea trunk, go to the train station, buy a ticket, and be on his way in a matter of days. But he did not do that. There was Greta.

To Karl, a future that included Greta meant they would be married. Was such a commitment possible? Karl felt there were certain requirements a man had to be able to meet before entering into a marriage. One was the ability to support a wife and ultimately children. He did not meet that test in any kind of scenario that he could think of. If they went west together, he would be in about the same situation as when he arrived in Baltimore. In a strange environment with no obvious means of earning a livelihood. If he stayed in Baltimore, he would have to improve his current situation, and he would be giving up his dream of being a landowner in America.

Greta wasn't as concerned. "Maybe you don't have much now, money, things like that. But you are ambitious, you have potential, dreams, a goal. That is more than a lot of men have. You will do alright, no matter what you do."

"You can't live on ambition or dreams."

"But you need them to be anybody in America."

Karl had grown fond of Greta. He was sure he loved her, but this was mixed up with other concerns and desires pushing and pulling him. He feared he was not prepared either to take on the responsibilities of marriage, regardless of Greta's confidence in his abilities or potential, or to give up his dream to go west.

*       *       *       *

It was the middle of March when Kermit and Pete surprised Karl by telling him that they would be leaving Baltimore soon for Chicago. This was an interesting turn of events. Karl had always imagined announcing his departure to the butchers, but now they were the ones telling him that they were leaving.

"Chicago, what's in Chicago?"

Kermit answered, "Where is Chicago? That's what we asked when some packing plant man came and talked to us. He wanted to hire us to go to Chicago, to train workers in a new kind of butchering."

"He tells us this city out west was only a little town a few years ago, and now it's bigger than Baltimore and growing like crazy. Just about every railroad that goes west goes through Chicago. If you want to build a big slaughter house, you do it in Chicago. The railroads can bring in animals from every direction and ship the meat out in every direction. The same thing that works for slaughtering works for everything else. Everything goes through Chicago. We talked to other people, they say the same thing. Everything goes through Chicago."

"What can be new about butchering?"

"They are building a really huge plant where they will be killing thousands of animals a day. There aren't enough master butchers in the world to handle the numbers they are talking about. So they want to train men fresh off the boat how to do one thing over and over. Stick it, scrape it, pull out the guts, trim, and cut. Each person does one thing over and over all day long. You get enough men, each doing one thing and pretty soon you have the whole animal butchered in a few minutes, and in another few minutes you have another one butchered."

"You know how to do that?"

"Well, they are going to pay us twice as much we are making now. They must think we know something. You said you were going to go west. Why not go to Chicago? The packing plants will be hiring a lot of men, good wages."

That was a new idea and Karl's mind started to work on it. If he was going west, why Omaha? Originally it was because his soldier friend, Hans, had relatives in Omaha. But since Hans was killed at Sedan, there was really no longer a reason for Karl to go to Omaha. It made sense when Hans was in the plans, but now, why not Chicago? Both cities were in the direction he wanted to go. Maybe Chicago would be a better place to work and save the money he needed.

Karl talked to Heinrich about the Chicago idea. He asked if Heinrich had ever heard anything about Chicago.

Heinrich had heard something. "I heard they had a big fire there last fall, burned up most of the town. Why?"

"I'm thinking that maybe I should go to Chicago instead of Omaha."

"Why?" Heinrich asked again. "It just burned down."

Karl didn't know about the fire, but he did know what the master butchers had told him. Karl repeated all that he had heard about Chicago. He added, "Maybe that is a place where jobs are looking for men."

Heinrich considered that for a while. "Chicago, how much does it cost to get to Chicago?"

"Seven dollars, about half what it would cost to get to Omaha."

"That's in my price range, I have seven dollars. Maybe I'll go with you."

Going to Chicago was now filling Karl's mind to the exclusion of almost everything else, even his obsession over Greta Whatever other plans he made, they would have to fit into the framework of going to Chicago. He was trying to fit Greta into that framework. Did he have to make a choice? Chicago or Greta?

Not having a better alternative, he talked to Heinrich about the dilemma.

"I want to go to Chicago, and I want to be with Greta. I don't know if I can do both."

"Don't think you are talking to the right person. Maybe a bartender or minister could help. You could flip a penny."

"I'm trying to be serious."

"Me too, but you know, when it comes to women, men don't need advice. If a man is ready to go through hellfire and floods for a woman, with no thought for the consequences, he's hooked. Advice of any kind will not change his mind. If he is hemming and hawing, then he is just looking at the bait."

"You think I am hemming and hawing?"

Heinrich laughed, avoiding a direct answer. "Women make life messy, God bless them."

Karl obtained information on train schedules to Chicago and worked on other details for making a move to the west. He was proceeding down a path without having solved the Greta dilemma, nor was he keeping her informed of his plans. He had purchased the tickets and he and Heinrich would be departing for Chicago the following week. Things had reached a point where Karl had to reveal his intentions.

Greta and Karl would be attending the English class on Sunday. Karl would have to tell her then.

On Sunday, a touch of spring was in the air when Karl and Greta walked to the English class. Tulips and daffodils were putting on a show and the budding trees were ready to burst. Greta was unusually restrained and Karl was quieter than usual. Karl was agonizing over how he was going to tell Greta that he and Heinrich would be leaving for Chicago next weekend. He was finding revealing his plans to Greta one of the hardest things he ever had to do. He could not bring up the subject during the class. It would have to be done on the way home.

They stopped at the Italian restaurant. This is where Karl would have to tell her. He could not procrastinate any further.

Antonia greeted them as they arrived.

"Gooda evening, the same?"

"The same."

They sat down at a corner table. Antonia brought two cups of coffee and a small pitcher of cream.

They added cream to the thick black coffee. Karl took a sip and nervously fingered his cup. He heard himself talking. His words seemed to come from a voice that was not a part of him.

"Greta, I am going to go west, to Chicago. Next Saturday, Heinrich is going with me. I have thought about this a lot, and it's what I have to do.

Greta's expression did not reveal a response to his announcement. She was silent for a long moment. "I am not surprised," she said finally. "I had that feeling. A woman knows. You have not been the same the past few weeks. That has always been your plan. Why should I be surprised?"

Karl was relieved that Greta was taking his decision so calmly. "You understand?"

"I understand. I knew that you never gave up that dream."

"I have very strong feelings about you. You know that."

"I know that."

"I wish the circumstances were different."

"Karl, you have helped me through this past winter. It would have been hard without you. You have helped me to understand that I need to help myself. My mother and I need to plan and dream like you have. We already have plans. The man that owns the business Herman runs, he has lots of money, other businesses. He has talked to us about running another green grocery. He knows we do all the work around the store, that we know the business better than Herman does. You don't have to worry about us in that way. I'll never forget this winter, the walks and talks. We had a lot of good times together."

Karl agreed. "We even learned some English."

Greta laughed. "And more."

Karl felt strangely expansive. "Let's celebrate our friendship, the good times we have had. Antonia, do you have any wine?"

"Of course, a red Toscana, good but reasonable. Fifty cents."

Karl gulped, but recovered. "Good, we will have that."

Antonia uncorked the red Toscana and had Karl sample it. They toasted each other, their friendship, each other's future.

Then they walked out into the fresh spring evening, realizing that this was probably the last time they would be together.

Karl walked all the way back to the store with Greta, remarking, "Herman can go to hell."

They lingered in the store doorway, embraced and kissed.

"We are parting as friends?" Karl asked.

"More than friends."

Karl agreed. "More than friends."

Karl walked back to the rooming house. He was elated at the way things had worked out. Yet he could feel a yearning ache in his chest. It was an ache that only time could cure.

# CHAPTER 8

▼

# TRAIN TO CHICAGO

The Baltimore and Ohio railroad operating out of Baltimore, like just about every other railroad company in the country, had passenger service to Chicago. Karl and Heinrich boarded the B & O at the Camden Station, leaving for Chicago at ten p.m. on a Saturday in early April, 1872. Their trunks had been checked into a baggage car, and they carried only their coats and two paper sacks filled with enough food to last for the trip.

There had been a choice of coach or Pullman cars. They didn't know what Pullman meant, but when they heard the price difference, coach seven dollars, Pullman twelve dollars, they didn't need to know any more.

The coach car had bench seats running along both sides and a narrow aisle down the middle. The seats could be adjusted to allow back to back seating or to have two seats facing each other. When seats were facing each other, a table top could be set up between them, an arrangement that provided an opportunity to become intimately acquainted with total strangers during an extended trip. There was one washroom facility in each car. Heat came in the form of two coal-burning stoves, one at each end. Three kerosene lamps, spaced evenly over the aisle, furnished dim lighting. A Negro porter made sure everyone found their seats, and kept the fires going and the lamps lit.

Both Karl and Heinrich wanted to be near the window to see as much of America as they could during the daylight hours, so they sat facing each other near the window. They were soon joined by a heavy-set man with a clean shaven lip and bearded jowls.

"Call me Joe," he said as he parked a bag under the seat. "And who might I have the pleasure of riding with?" Hearing the German accent, he engaged them in butchered but understandable German. Joe said he spoke several languages, including English, none of them well. The fourth seat in the two-bench compartment remained unfilled.

"So what's your business?" Joe asked, addressing whoever wanted to answer.

Karl volunteered that they were on their way to Chicago, where they expected to find work in the meat-packing business.

"Going to Chicago, Chicago, the can-do town. Well, good, so am I. We can stay together all the way. I travel on these trains all the time, good to have company. Do you fellows play cards? Like a little poker to pass the time?"

Both Karl and Heinrich demurred. They were familiar with the game, but did not feel they had any money to risk.

A fourth passenger arrived to fill the remaining seat. A young man, probably in his early thirties. He carried an overnight bag.

"I'm getting off at Cumberland, not far down the road. Not used to these cramped coaches. Take the Pullman whenever I can, but makes no sense on a short trip."

Joe introduced himself. "Ride the trains all the time, never the Pullmans."

"Why? The only way to travel if you're going any distance."

"I usually stay up most of the night, so for me it doesn't make sense for any trip. If you are in a sleeper car, they all get changed over to beds. If you want to stay up, you are out of luck."

Karl was able to follow most of what was being said and asked, "What do you mean by Pullman, 'sleepers'?"

Joe explained, "During the day they look a lot like this car, only nicer, but at night, they are converted over to beds for sleeping. They are made up into bunks stacked two to three high along each side with a curtain pulled over the front for privacy. If you are going a long distance, want to get some rest, that's the way to travel."

It was dark, so it was not possible to see much, but it was obvious that the train was traveling through a hilly area. "Appalachians," somebody said. Joe had wandered off somewhere and Heinrich had one whole bench seat to himself, so he fixed his coat to make a pillow and laid down to get some sleep. Karl didn't have that option. He remained seated and gazed out into the darkness. The clicking of the train wheels made him aware that he was again moving away from the familiar and towards the goal that was pulling him. The throbbing of the SS *Ohio* had carried him away from his home, and now the clicking of the rails was carrying him away from his first stop in America and a woman he loved. The thought of Greta brought back good memories and strong desires. They were desires that would be unfulfilled and he could feel a sense of loss. The click of the rails soothed his mind. The inexorable power of the train was carrying him into the unknown. It was out of his hands now.

The businessman going to Cumberland got off the train, opening up the possibility for Karl to make his seat into a makeshift bed. He followed Heinrich's example, made a pillow out of his coat, and was soon asleep.

The next morning found the train in Wheeling, West Virginia. Joe had returned sometime during the night and had deprived Heinrich of his makeshift bed. Joe was now sleeping sitting in an upright position on the hard bench seat. He slept most of the forenoon and roused himself about dinnertime. Karl and Heinrich were working on the contents of their food sacks. Joe didn't have any lunch with him.

"Want a sandwich?" Karl asked.

"No thanks, I will take my dinner in the dining car."

Heinrich raised an eyebrow. "I thought coach passengers weren't supposed to eat in the dining car."

"Rules don't apply to everyone. A little money can change the rules. Works wonders with porters."

Karl and Heinrich had walked through the Pullman section the previous evening. They wanted to find out what could make the fare so much higher. It was pretty impressive. Bedrooms on rails. They had never seen anything like that in Germany.

During the afternoon Karl and Heinrich watched the scenery go by. It was a grey day with rays of sunlight poking through occasionally. Soon after the train left West Virginia, the land had flattened out. There were many farms, small towns, and scattered hardwood forests. As the train traveled west and north the forest land decreased and more land was under cultivation. Many neat farmsteads dotted the landscape.

Joe was reading a book and dozing off occasionally. Towards evening he started to perk up. He had supper in the dining car while Karl and Heinrich finished off a loaf of bread and some summer sausage.

As daylight faded, Joe seemed to grow restless. The previous night he had been away somewhere until late, but tonight he was hanging around.

"You fellows said you were poker players. Ever hear of the game blackjack?" he asked.

Karl and Heinrich were not sure.

"Let me show you the game. No gambling, I'll just show you how it goes. Let's set up the table."

Joe took a deck of cards shuffled them. Joe's hands were large and blunt, but Karl was amazed at how smoothly he handled the cards. The cards seemed to dance in his hands. They played through the deck a couple of times. Blackjack seemed like a simple enough game and Karl and Heinrich soon had the hang of it.

"You wonder what I do for a living?" Joe asked. "Well, I'm a gambler, that's how I make my living. That's why I'm always on the trains, that's where I gamble. There's a fellow I played with last night, wants to play again. I took him for a little and he wants to get it back. I mentioned knowing a couple of people who would like to play with us tonight. Those people are you fellows."

"Ya?"

"I think you will want to play."

"Why?"

"When I tell you the deal."

Both Karl and Heinrich were a little leery of this fast talking apparent con-man, but agreed to have "the deal" explained.

"Well, I like you guys, like to have you in the game, so what I will do is advance both of you five silver dollars. You will get to keep the five dollars if you don't lose it, but I get any winnings. How is that for a deal? You could make yourselves five dollars each, can't lose anything, and I get any winnings."

Karl and Heinrich looked at each other.

Heinrich asked, "Why would you do that?"

"I can see you fellows are quick with cards."

It didn't make sense to Heinrich, "Wouldn't that be like three against one? Would that be fair?"

"It gives me three chances to lose, it's a game of chance. What is cheating about that?"

Karl and Heinrich wanted to talk it over and went out to the walkway between cars. It was hard to converse because of the noise and wind, but it was private.

"The guy is a con man." Karl stated flatly.

"Sure he is, but five dollars is a lot of money. We are just two gullible immigrants, we don't know what is going on. Joe is the guy that is hanging out. We can go along for the ride, duck if things get messy."

"I don't like the sound of it. Americans get real upset when someone puts the fix on them."

"Look, we keep our eyes open. If anything gets iffy, we get out of there."

Reluctantly, Karl agreed to play.

Joe introduced the gentleman that was interested in a game of blackjack. From his accent, it was apparent that he was a southerner. He had a gaunt, mean look. Roger Clemings was his name.

"This is Karl and Heinrich, recent German immigrants, don't know much English, but they are interested in learning the game, so they will sit in for a few hands if it is okay. I can talk enough German to keep them up to speed if they get confused."

Karl had to suppress a smile. Actually he and Heinrich understood quite a lot of English by this time, thanks to Karl's English class and Heinrich's exposure to English on his job. But tonight they were German rubes who barely understood English and who wanted to learn the game of blackjack.

Joe was dealing. The game moved along at a reasonable pace and the winning cards seemed to be moving around the table in a normal way. Joe pulled a bottle of sipping whiskey out of his satchel with four glasses and poured a round. Drinking outside of the dining or lounge cars was prohibited, but again, using Joe's technique, a little tip for the porter, this was not a problem. Sipping corn whiskey was a new experience for Karl. It had a sharp hard-edged smell, burned all the way down, but turned into a warm glow after settling into his stomach. Something he could get used to.

Roger had been a captain in the Confederate Army. On the right, though losing side, according to Roger. Pickett's army. He was wounded and damn lucky to be alive after Gettysburg. Roger was going to do some business in Chicago with some damn Yankees. Did the Germans know anything about the Franco-Prussian war? Roger, in addition to being a veteran, was a war buff and followed the Franco-Prussian war closely. Karl admitted that he had fought at Sedan. Roger showed a flicker of surprise. Maybe these Germans weren't the boobs he had assumed them to be.

The night wore on. There was more sipping whiskey. With the passing of time, the winnings seemed to be accumulating in the direction of the gullible immigrants, at the expense of Roger and Joe. The odds seemed to be working against Roger and he was starting to show signs of exasperation.

Joe sympathized with Roger. "If it wasn't for bad luck, I wouldn't be having any luck at all. I'm holding my own, but can't seem to pull ahead. How do you Krauts do it? Maybe you know more than you admit."

Heinrich played his part. "Vel ve didn't know much ven ve first come here. You vouldn't believe how dumb ve ver."

Karl added, "Sometimes, I tink ve are still dumb."

Roger didn't seem to be buying it. There was something about the game that he didn't like, and he was down, way down.

Karl had to agree that something did seem funny about the game. It seemed he and Heinrich were extremely fortunate in the cards they were getting.

"Let's change the cards," Roger stated as he pulled a new deck out of his coat pocket and threw it on the table.

"Fine with me, sounds like a good idea," Joe agreed. "Okay with you fellows?" Joe asked, giving Karl and Heinrich a glance. They shrugged, not seeming to care.

The new deck did not seem to help matters. Roger was becoming more agitated as his losses mounted. He was obviously losing more than he could afford.

Roger reached the end of his patience when Karl split two aces and made twenty-one on both of them. Roger's background suggested he was a man of action. He reached inside the top coat he was wearing and pulled out a mean looking derringer. The arm holding the derringer was laid on the table, with the gun pointed at Joe's chest, not more than a foot away.

"Just count out the amount I brought to this game, and we will call it a night," Roger hissed.

Joe was a big man, a little on the heavy side, but he was surprisingly quick. He didn't hesitate. With his one arm he deflected the hand holding the derringer away from him and with the other hand came down with a closed fist on the gun holding arm, causing the gun to drop to the floor. In a moment the two men were rolling in the car's passageway, attracting all kinds of attention from the other car passengers.

Heinrich scooped up his stack and motioned for Karl to do the same. They headed out of the car. When they got to the door, a porter and a fellow with a badge were coming into the car. Heinrich and Karl kept going until they found some empty seats two cars down from where they had been riding. The rest of the night they sat there, wide-eyed and expecting Joe or Roger or somebody to accost them at any minute. But nobody did.

The half light of early dawn revealed that the train was traveling through flat farm land on one side and a large body of water on the other.

"What is that, an ocean?" Heinrich asked.

Karl knew his geography well enough to know that it wasn't an ocean. "We must be close to Chicago. Chicago is on a big lake."

The sun was pushing over the horizon as the train pulled into the station in Chicago, and the passengers were soon disembarking. Karl remembered he had left his coat in the car where the poker game had been played. He wanted to go back and retrieve it before getting off the train.

Heinrich was ready to get off the train at the first opportunity. "Forget it, it's worn out anyway."

Karl was reluctant to leave the coat behind. "It's my Prussian army coat."

"Good enough reason to leave it."

"I'll go back, see if it is still there."

"If you see Roger or Joe, forget the damn coat."

Karl went back to the door of the car they had been in, looked through the glass and saw his coat still laying in the window rack. Otherwise the car was completely empty.

When they disembarked in Chicago, Karl had his coat, and they were a lot better off financially and a little more worldly than they had been when they left Baltimore.

The station they had disembarked at seemed to be in the middle of a reconstruction project. Heinrich sniffed the air. "I think I can still smell the smoke. This place must have burned down in the big fire."

They decided to count the money that had fallen their way the previous night. Karl counted his gains at thirty dollars and Heinrich counted thirty-seven dollars.

After finishing the counting, Heinrich noted that he had considerably more money than Karl. "Should we split it evenly, like good proletarians?"

"No," Karl insisted. "You won that fair and square. It's yours"

"I'm not too sure about the fair and square part of it. If it were fair and square, we wouldn't be counting this money. I wonder what happened to Joe and the captain?"

"Probably tipped a porter and got everything straightened out."

"Don't think so. Lucky to get out of there with our skins whole, not to mention the money."

"Amen to that."

# CHAPTER 9

▼

# CHICAGO 1872

When Karl and Heinrich emerged from the train station, they confronted what Joe had called the "can-do" city. A quick look certainly indicated a lot of can-do going on. Construction was evident everywhere. It appeared that the center of the city had been leveled and was being completely rebuilt. In the meantime, the business of the city was being conducted as usual. It was as though the hectic business pace of the city had not slowed down, but it had only added a layer of reconstruction on top of its normally frenetic activities.

It was early morning and they figured they should be able to make it to the packing plant before the end of the day.

They got directions from a construction worker on the street.

"Go to Ashland, down about five blocks, then south on Ashland until you get there. You will know it when you're there."

They started walking, carrying their trunks on their shoulders. They found Ashland, then started south.

The streets were crowded with shoppers, shopkeepers, office workers, construction workers, and construction materials. There were horse-drawn wagons, carts and buggies going in all directions. Everyone seemed to be in a hurry.

Karl was impressed. "Compared to this, Baltimore seems like a country village."

Sections of Ashland were covered with cobblestones, but mostly it was dirt. Torn up by the construction going on. More accurately it was mud, because of the recent rains and there were holes where you could lose a horse.

They continued south on Ashland for some distance, but didn't seem to be getting anywhere. They were still in the middle of a city being rebuilt. From what they could tell, Ashland Avenue went south as far as the eye could see, flat and straight as an arrow.

Karl was beginning to question the notion that they could walk to the stock-yards. He had noticed a number of buggies that appeared to be for hire going up and down the streets and suggested they hire a ride. Heinrich, who had been thinking along the same lines, readily agreed.

Karl, always on the alert to save a penny, spotted a single-box wagon with steel-rimmed, wooden-spoked wheels, pulled by two thin, mismatched horses. The sideboards were bleached white from age and neglect, and the box was half-filled with scrap material and garbage. Karl hailed the driver, an elderly Negro sitting on a springboard seat mounted near the front of the wagon.

"Haul us to the stockyards?"

The driver looked the two young men over. "Maybe."

"Going that way?"

"Maybe."

"How much?"

"Dollar."

"Sounds like a lot."

"Worth it."

"How far?"

"A long ways."

"How about seventy five cents?"

"Costs a dollar."

"Damn it, Karl, give the man a dollar."

They piled their trunks into the single-box wagon, trying to avoid the garbage.

The driver giddy-upped the team and they started south on Ashland. He wore an old bowler hat, grey with dust, oversized black wool trousers, and a grey coat.

"Where you all from?"

"Baltimore."

"Baltimore, now I had folks back tet way. Jes git here?"

"This morning."

"Dets jes for sure, I jes git here after ta war."

Karl asked the driver if he had been burned out by the big fire.

"Nope, lived south fer nuf. Close, dats fo sur."

They were moving south on Ashland, and after a while were out of the burned out part of the city. The building types changed from stores and offices to tenements. People crowded the streets. There seemed to be a lot of litter around.

Their driver turned up his nose. "Dirty Irish, mosly."

Karl and Heinrich exchanged glances. Karl asked, "Many Germans around?"

The driver laughed. "Lotsa beer drinkers."

The driver was guiding his horses around the biggest mud holes while he talked. The traffic was thinning and he was making better time. Off in the distance they could see a cloud of smoke and steam rising.

They continued to move at a steady pace for some time, and Karl began to wonder how long it was going to take. They had not eaten since last night and food was becoming an issue.

"How much farther?" he asked the driver.

"Close."

"How close?"

In the distance large structures were becoming apparent in the place where the smoke and steam were billowing up into the sky.

The driver gestured towards the smoke and emerging structures.

"Dets where we goin. You fellas goin ta work der?"

"That's the plan."

"Dets not fo me."

"Why's that?"

"Dets fo young men, can't do det no moe. Usta work from sunup to sunset in the cotton fields. No mo."

"Cotton, down South."

"Dets right, down South, no mo, dets for sure, no mo."

As they drew closer to the looming structures a heavy odor that had a hint of sweetness became apparent, and it grew stronger as they approached their destination. The details of a mammoth building many stories high, rumbling with the sound of work being done, was emerging from the steam and smoke. Next to the plant were animal pens that went as far as the eye could see and from which they heard a constant bellowing and squealing.

It was an overpowering sight. Karl had been expecting something different than a normal butchering operation, but not anything like this. He was familiar with butchering as done by his brother in Prussia, and with butchering as done in the small slaughtering house he had worked at in Baltimore. Nothing in his past experience prepared him for what he was seeing here.

"The butchers in Baltimore told me that this was something different."

Heinrich agreed. "There should be some jobs in a place as big as this. But where do you start to find them?"

"I think we start with something to eat. I'm starved."

The driver asked, "Where you want off?"

"Someplace we can get something to eat."

"Has to go Back of the Yards den."

They continued down Ashland, the stock yards on their left, the huge plant and some smaller buildings on their right, until they got to 47th Street.

The appearance of the Back of the Yards neighborhood was that of disorder. A mix of one- and two-story wood-frame buildings, tenements, cottages, bars, and stores competed for space. The same heavy odor with a hint of sweetness pervaded the neighborhood and the bellowing and squealing from the yards was still audible. The buildings did not appear old and probably weren't, but many were already leaning or sagging.

Heinrich guessed that they must be building for another fire. "And it better happen pretty quick."

Karl felt apprehensive. This did not have the feel of a pleasant neighborhood.

There was a place on the corner that looked like it might have food. They decided to take a chance and had the driver drop them off. They stepped down to a dirt street muddy from recent rains and dodged puddles on the way to the front door.

It stood by itself on the corner, a long, narrow gabled-roofed, one-story building with wood, vertical-plank siding. Wooden laths covered the cracks between the planks. There was an entry at the narrow front end of the building, and on either side of the entry were windows that looked like oversized house windows. A small, faded American flag hung from a broom handle projecting out above the entry. A wooden sign over the right front window had a yellow background and a green shamrock in the upper right-hand corner. The word "Flanagan's" was painted across the sign in green letters.

Karl sounded out the word and noted the shamrock. "Irish, I would guess," he said. "At least they should have some beer."

The front door opened into a square-shaped area filled with half a dozen tables with red and white checked tablecloths. A short bar with four stools and some standing room ran across the back. Behind the bar was a wall, which probably hid a kitchen. At ten a.m. the two of them were the only customers.

They sat their trunks down and settled into chairs at a table with a good view of the depressing scene in front of the building.

A woman came out of the back and walked over to their table. She had a purposeful stride, a strong, almost manly build, dark straight hair pulled back, smooth skin, and dark brown eyes.

"What will it be?" she asked.

"Do you serve food?" Heinrich asked.

"And beer and whiskey, and whatever else you might need." She glanced at their trunks. "You fellows new here?"

"Got here today."

"Going to work in the butcher business?"

"What else?"

She laughed. "Welcome to slaughter city. I'm Maria. We have borscht, pita bread stuffed with meat, vegetables."

"Don't sound very Irish?"

"Probably as Irish as you two Krauts."

"You don't look very Irish either."

"Stanka, Maria Stanka is the name, same last name as my mother. We run the place."

"Why the Irish name?"

"Lots of Irish in the neighborhood. That was the name on it when we took it over."

Heinrich decided, "I'll have your borscht, and a big glass of beer."

Karl followed suit.

Maria left to get their order.

Karl watched her walk away. "Kind of sassy."

"That's for sure, but you know, she might be able to give us some ideas about where to get a room."

They queried her when she got back.

"Everyone around here works in the slaughterhouses or in the yards. Lots of places to stay up and down the street. There is one place, two doors down the street, nothing fancy, but after killing hogs all day, who cares? Sullivan owns it. He has an office right next door. Stop in there."

"First we have to find out if we can get a job."

"Don't worry, they are hiring anybody who's warm."

"After the borscht, we should qualify. What would it cost to leave our trunks here for a while?"

"Your business, for the next two years."

"That's reasonable, any idea where you apply for a job?"

"There's a big plant, they just finished building it, still working on some parts. You had to come by it if you were on Ashland. They should have signs."

They walked back up Ashland towards the big plant. Lots of construction debris lay about, and scaffolding covered parts of the building where men were still working on it. They approached guard standing by one of the gates.

"We're looking for work," Karl stated.

"Follow the fence, until you come to the next gate. Go in there."

They followed the guard's directions and came to a place with a sign over the entrance that said "Entry, Employment Applicants." There was a line of men that was moving into the building and they joined them. The line moved right along and they were soon in a large room in front of a counter where a stocky man looked the two of them over.

The man was talking, as if to himself. "Mm, maybe a little light for the killing floor, the hog cutting room should work." He hesitated, then added, "Go over to table four."

There were six tables placed about the room, each with a large number to identify it. Karl and Heinrich walked over to table four where a man was sitting with some paper and cards strewn about. There were no chairs for the applicants to sit on.

"You want to be cutters, eh?" the man asked without looking up. He was small, wearing a rumpled coat and pants and a shirt open at the neck that had been white at one time, but now had a yellow cast to it. In his mouth was a cheap, strong-smelling cigar that had gone out long ago.

"Your name?"

Karl and Heinrich each gave him their names.

"Can you spell that?" The man wrote the information on partially filled-out cards and in a ledger that lay in front of him.

"Okay, you report at gate eight tomorrow morning at six. Show them this card," the man said as he handed each a card.

Heinrich interrupted, "How many hours, how much will we be paid, what kind of work will we be doing?"

The man gave him a "Who cares?" kind of look," but responded, "Cutting up hogs, usually twelve hours, depending on the size of the kill, a dollar fifty cents summer, two dollars winter, six days a week. Next."

They walked out a little surprised at how quickly and informally everything had been handled.

"Karl, I think we have a job. I'm pretty sure I can handle the smell of this place, but how do I know, how do they know if I can do the work?"

"I think all they care about is that you are able to stand up and are strong enough to do the work."

"No need for brains?"

"That's for sure, so that won't be a problem."

The overwhelming size of the plant, the indifferent attitude of the people in the hiring hall, and the depressing appearance of the neighborhood was bothering Karl. The pay, a dollar fifty cents in the summer, two dollars in the winter, was more than twice as much as either one had been earning in Baltimore. That was the incentive. Was it worth it? Karl felt he could put up with what seemed to be oppressive work and living conditions if it was temporary and got him to his goal.

"Maybe it won't seem so bad after we get used to it," Karl stated encouragingly. "Moving and doing something different always takes getting used to. Remember leaving Germany, the ship, Baltimore."

"Ya, change is hard."

"Do you understand why pay is higher in winter?"

"No, that's strange."

They checked out the rooming house that Maria had recommended. It was a two-story, wood-frame building with clapboard siding. Sullivan, the owner, showed them the room and other accommodations. The building was almost new, but when they entered they were hit with an old apartment house odor. There was the litter in the hallways and the neglected maintenance they had become accustomed to in Baltimore. There were six rooms down, six rooms up. The vacant room was on the second floor in the middle. It was a single room the same size of their Baltimore apartment, furnished in a similar way. Its only window looked out on the shingled roof of the building next to it. The distance between the two buildings was less than three feet. On the back of the tenement was a nice feature: porches that were six feet wide and ran the width of the building on both levels.

Sanitation was provided in a shed out back, and consisted of a toilet and a couple of tubs for washing clothes, or bathing if one was so inclined. A small stove to be used for heating water and for warmth in the winter, sat in the corner. An unpleasant odor permeated the inside of the shed, so strong that it overwhelmed the foul-smelling atmosphere in the area.

Maria was right, it was nothing fancy, but representative of what was available in the neighborhood. They decided to take it, six dollars a month each.

# CHAPTER 10

▼

# THE JOB

The next morning at six a.m. they arrived at gate eight as directed. A group of men had gathered and were milling around, not knowing what to do next. A man walked up, and shouted, "Everyone assigned to the killing floor, follow me." Another man showed up and called for meat cutters to follow him.

Heinrich nudged Karl. "I think that's us."

A group of twenty would-be meat cutters, all new hires, were led up four levels to the middle of the immense plant. They entered a large room where five men in white coats were standing around.

One of the men, wearing a necktie, addressed them.

"Today you are in class. You are going to learn about cutting meat, and at the same time we will be working out what each of you will be doing. We'll work on this until we get a line moving. Joe," he pointed to the smallest man wearing a white coat, "He's a tool man, he will be telling you about knives, meat axes, meat saws, how you use them, where you get them. Kurt and Johann are master butchers. They are going to be telling each one of you what you are going to be doing and how to do it. And Fred, the guy with the clip board, he is going to be writing everything down, so we don't forget what the hell we are doing when we finally get it figured out."

The man with the tie left and the tool man took over.

"You will have sharp tools all the time. The tools you pick up first thing in the morning will be sharp. If one breaks or gets too dull, get a new one. Mostly you will be using knives in this work. Some meat axes and saws."

"Be careful, the knives are razor sharp. That is the way it has to be. They will cut anything that gets in the way, including fingers. I know plenty of four-finger, no-fingered cutters. When you are going to make a cut, don't have your fingers spread out. Make a fist." He grabbed a piece of meat and demonstrated. "Fortunately, I have never seen a cutter cut a finger off his knife hand, always the holding hand. Just bandage it up and keep cutting."

Many of the men, whose English was marginal, probably didn't understand much of what was being said, but it didn't matter as long as they knew where to pick up the right tools for their station.

The two master butchers took over next. Both had heavy German accents, and reminded Karl of the master butchers he worked with in Baltimore. One of the butchers explained the plan for the day. Each worker was going to be assigned a station along the long conveyer that ran through the middle of the room. Each worker would make certain cuts on the hog carcass that would be moving along the conveyer.

"Today you will be learning what those cuts are, what is supposed to happen at each station. First we have to figure what those cuts are ourselves. There will be a little experimenting today."

The white-coated man with the writing board was writing as the master butchers talked and worked.

Karl knew enough about the business to understand what the master butchers were doing. They had been trained to handle one animal at a time with each butcher or team of butchers doing all the tasks: killing, cleaning, and dissecting each animal from start to finish. Now they had to break down everything they normally did into individual, simple steps to be done by unskilled workers.

The hog carcasses they would be working on had been hanging in a cold room for a couple of days and had been cleaned, beheaded, and cut in half.

The carcasses moved into the cutting room on hangers. One of the bigger men was selected to lift the animals off the hooks and lay them on the conveyer. The conveyer was engaged to move the animal to the first station, where two men, one at the head end and one at the tail end were stationed. The master butchers instructed the two cutters as to what they were supposed to do with the carcass. The carcass was moved to the next station, and two more cutters were given their instructions. This continued until all the stations were occupied.

The butchers were making adjustments as they assigned tasks to each station. Finally all stations were in place. The conveyer moved one station at a time as the butchers continued to train the workers and adjust the process. This went on until early afternoon, when the butchers announced that they would try a run with the conveyer moving continuously, Each station would have to complete its cuts while the animal was in front of the station. The line was moving, very slowly. The new meat cutters were getting the job done and the process, just developed, was functioning. They kept the line running for about an hour, and then it was shut down.

It was the middle of the afternoon when the newly trained cutters were let go for the day.

Leaving the plant, Heinrich looked up at the afternoon sun. "Nice hours."

"Ya, enjoy it. They can't afford to run this plant part-time for long."

"Think I got my cuts down."

"You know they will start speeding that line up."

"I know."

Things continued in the same manner for the rest of the week and they never worked longer than nine hours on any given day. More adjustments were made to the line. Each day the line was moving a little faster. Towards the end of the week, the workers would sometimes find themselves struggling to finish their task before the next animal arrived. Their knives were moving faster and faster.

After the first two weeks, the German butchers were gone, and in their place was a large loud Irishman with a red beard and a ruddy complexion, who introduced himself as Dan.

"I'm your supervisor. My job is to get the day's production done, get it done right. Cutters are more skilled than most people in this place, so if you don't make it to work some day, we probably won't be able to get a new man to fill in right away, so the line will slow down. Too many missed days and you will be replaced, understand? Okay, get to your places, let's move it."

The line started up, moving faster than the previous week. From the start, Karl was pressing to keep up. He would be working on his part as it moved by, but sometimes the next carcass was almost out of his reach by the time he got to it and another carcass was passing his station. There wasn't a moment to relax; the carcasses just kept coming. Dan kept walking up and down the line, warning lagging workers to pick up the pace. Carcasses would occasionally get by a station, and the line would have to be stopped. This would set Dan off yelling and questioning the offending worker's ancestry. By lunchtime Karl felt drained. He ate his lunch and tried to rest. At one p.m. they started again, and Karl struggled to keep up. At three p.m. Dan shut down for the day. They had spent eight hours on the line, and Karl couldn't imagine how he could have worked for another four hours, or what was supposed to be a normal day.

Heinrich was dragging also. "I don't know if I'm going to be able to do this. Not sure I can work twelve hours at the pace we were going today, or ten hours for that matter." They had one ten-hour day during the week and finished in nine hours on Saturday. A couple of the cutters were replaced, Karl and Heinrich were hurting, but their young bodies were adjusting to the task. In a way, it was becoming a challenge, kind of a game. They would prove that they could stand with the best of them and take whatever they threw at them. In the next few weeks, their skills increased and their bodies adapted to the work. Eventually they were averaging twelve hours on most days. Karl was saving ten dollars a month most months. But he intensely disliked the work and the oppressive living conditions, and sometimes wondered if what he was striving for justified the means to achieve it.

# CHAPTER 11

▼

# LIVING IN THE BACK OF THE YARDS

Karl's memory of the Baltimore experience was filtered by time and distance, but in retrospect, it seemed the move to Chicago was a step backwards with regards to work and living conditions. And then there was Greta. Karl missed the Sundays spent with Greta. Nothing in his Chicago experience was compensating for the companionship Greta had provided. He missed the Baltimore church and its ties to the past. Karl had found a small missionary Lutheran congregation in the Back of the Yards neighborhood. It met in a rented meeting hall. There was no organ, only a tinny-sounding upright piano. The minister was young and enthusiastic, but not like the stern elder Lutheran ministers Karl was familiar with. After attending a few times, Karl did not return to the missionary congregation.

The first summer in Chicago introduced Karl and Heinrich to oppressive Midwestern heat waves, when summer heat and high humidity combined to make life at work, and in their apartment room, torturous. Eventually the heat and high humidity would generate horrendous summer storms with intense lighting and high winds that would break the heat wave. Then there would be a period of cooler temperatures and dryer air. The knowledge that the heat would eventually give way to more moderate conditions did not reduce the misery it created. The early mornings were tolerable, but by about noon the cutting room was hot and wringing wet. Karl and Heinrich would be soaked with sweat by the time the day was done, and then they had to go back to a room that was hardly habit-able. Even a breeze didn't help in the closely packed apartments. The back porch on their building became a refuge, where on the hottest nights they hauled out their mattresses and made it a bedroom. Hordes of mosquitos were preferable to the stagnant hot room.

While sitting on the back porch one hot night, Heinrich questioned Karl's decision to move to this part of the world.

Karl had to admit it was miserably hot. "But good for growing corn."

"They must grow a lot of corn in hell, if that's the case."

"If you were out in the country, in the fields, or under the shade of a tree, it wouldn't be so bad."

"But we aren't."

"I will be after a couple years of this."

"I'm beginning to see some sense in that dream of yours. Things can be miser-able, hopeless almost, and you are dreaming about how good things are going to be—someday. Even if it never happens you get to enjoy your dream."

The weather had moderated by early fall. They had become comfortable with the work pace, life was starting to feel tolerable. Then the line was speeded up again. Karl and Heinrich, being young and near their physical prime, were able to absorb this, but they were straining and near their limit.

They went on the winter pay schedule in October, and now understood the reason for the pay differential. Twelve hours was normal, there were no short days, and some days ran to fourteen hours.

They had started making a habit of stopping in at Flanagan's on Saturday nights for a beer, and after the speed-up they felt they really needed to make that stop.

Most saloons and restaurants were ethnic. The Irish went to Irish saloons, the Germans to German saloons, but Flanagan's had a mixed clientele. Maybe it was because the name of the place and the nationality of the owner were mixed up. Maybe it was because Flanagan's was located in a "no man's land" between ethnic enclaves. Whatever the reason, all ethnic groups felt welcome at Flanagan's.

Maria was always there. "What can I do for you boys tonight?" she asked as she wiped up their table. "The usual?"

"Ya," Karl replied. "One pitcher out of the tap and two glasses." For financial reasons, Karl limited his beer intake to a shared pitcher, once a week, maybe two pitchers if it had been an especially bad week.

Heinrich was not on such a rigid regimen and indulged a little more freely. He occasionally made the Saturday night dances at the Packers Hall and sometimes played penny-ante poker at O'Riley's, another ethnically mixed-up place. Heinrich, inspired by Karl, did put a little money away in the better months. He was not sure why he was saving the money but expected it would come in handy some day.

They were joined by Emil, another one of the original cutters on their line.

"Maria, another glass, and what the hell, another pitcher."

"Big spenders."

"Ya, and how much are you charging tonight?"

"More than any slaughterhouse worker could afford."

"That's not very much."

They got their beer and set about enjoying one of the few luxuries they could afford.

"Do you think she really…?"

"Nien."

"Who would buy it anyway?"

"That's the thing."

Emil changed the subject. "I don't know if I can handle the new speed-up. I'm hurting."

Karl was encouraging. "If you made it through the week, you will make it all right. It's the third day that tells the story. If you make it past the third day, you will make it all the way."

"You think so? The line has been up six months and this is the second speed-up. How much faster can we go?"

Heinrich was not sure he could go any faster. "Speed it up more and I'll be flying out the door. It's a chew-them-up, use-them-up, and spit-them-out kind of business."

Karl agreed. "We can do it. Just takes getting used to, but it's a young man's game, not the kind of work you spend your life doing. Not like my brother Walter, he's a butcher in Prussia, and he will do that the rest of his life. Not this kind of butcher business."

"So why do it?" Emil wanted to know. "We know we are being used up and we still do it. Are we dumb or something?"

"Sure we are," Heinrich answered. "It's hard to be smart when you only have dumb choices. It's the best job we can get, that's why, and you know, some men like it. They like to beat the line. They don't ever expect to slow down or get old. Then there's Karl, trying to save enough to homestead some land so he will only have to work six months of the year and get rich."

Karl laughed. "That's right, how did you know?"

"You been telling me about it every other day for the last two years, that's how."

The large kills and long days continued all winter and through most of the spring. As spring turned into their second summer, their work days shortened, and they started drawing summer pay. Then something unexpected happened. The plant went to a five-day week, sometimes less.

Some of the veterans in the business weren't surprised. Pete, the big Bohemian, had been around a while and explained, "Hell, we used to shut down in the summer altogether, before they built this plant with the big chiller. Couldn't keep the meat more than a day or two. Now it's just the supply that slows us down. Farmers are busy with other things in the summer. Hogs are getting ready, but aren't ready yet."

Karl couldn't remember any shortage of hogs the previous summer.

"That's because they were trying to figure out how to run this place. We weren't killing like we are now."

Karl had not been expecting or planning on this slowdown, and it had an immediate effect on his financial plans. His plans were based on six-day weeks. Anything less than that would upset his schedule.

# CHAPTER 12

▼

# SUMMER DOLDRUMS

Even though the summer slowdown upset Karl's plans, an extra day off was a luxury, a form of compensation for the lower pay. The first Saturday off, he slept in until the room temperature, driven up by the summer heat, forced him out. He moved out to the back porch, smoked his pipe and swatted the flies that seemed to thrive in the privy-filled alley. The scene from the back porch was now familiar, but having time to sit and contemplate it made him realize how ugly this neighborhood really was. The buildings, unpainted for the most part, were turning a uniform grey. There were no trees, grass, or paving. Just dirt, grey like the buildings. It was muddy or dusty, depending on the weather. The animal sounds and the odoriferous packing plant stench and stock yard smells permeated the neighborhood.

After Karl finished smoking his pipe, he was at a loss as to what to do next. Heinrich had just gotten up. He stretched as he came out to the porch.

"Looks like another hot one."

"What's your plan for a hot summer day?"

"I might go down to O'Riley's and play a little penney ante. Come along, something to do."

It would be something to do. Saloons offered about the only form of recreation in the neighborhood, and there were a lot of them. Karl didn't want to be spending too much of his diminished wages, but playing penny ante shouldn't set him back too far.

Compared to Flanagan's, O'Riley's was a large-scale operation. The first level of the two-story building was filled with tables and a bar ran the full length of one side wall. The saloon was open every day of the week. Ten in the morning until ten at night Sunday through Friday, and until two in the morning on Saturday night. There was a buffet that was open at noon. Customers could order food off a blackboard menu at any time. O'Riley's didn't run any gambling games, but private parties were permitted to gamble on the premises. Card games were going on from the time the place opened until it closed, and anyone interested in play-ing could soon find an opening.

The second level at O'Riley's was partitioned into a large number of small rooms. Most rooms were rented by the hour, while some were rented by the week or month by ladies that worked the tables.

Heinrich and Karl found room in a game of penny ante five-card draw.

Waiters would stop by every so often to take drink orders. Karl had his glass filled with draft beer several times.

Before it seemed possible, it was late afternoon.

Heinrich suggested they take their winnings and go over to Flanagan's and have something to eat.

"What winnings? I didn't notice you winning any more than I did. I'm down twenty cents."

"Just a way of talking."

It was Saturday evening, and as usual, Flanagan's was busy. Maria was more dressed up than usual. She had on a dress Karl had never seen her wear before and there was a glow in her cheeks that wasn't natural.

"What's the occasion?"

"I'm getting off tonight. Ma's got some help."

"To do what?"

"Going to Packers Hall with a couple of friends."

Heinrich had been there before. "Gets pretty rough sometimes."

"Sure does."

Heinrich turned to Karl, "How about that?"

"How about what?"

"Going to the Packers Hall."

"No, I'm so far into my savings now…"

Emil came in the door.

"Hey Emil," Heinrich called, "Come over here."

Emil ambled over. "Want to share a pitcher?"

"No, something bigger. We're going to Packers Hall. Want to go along?"

Karl gave Heinrich a puzzled look.

Emil wasn't sure. The last time he was there he just about got into a fight with some big Bohunk.

Heinrich coached, "Just for a little while, to check things out."

It was agreed. They would just check things out.

Packers Hall was what the name implied, a big hall used for Saturday night dances and rented out for special occasions. Like Flanagan's, dance halls were places where there was an ethnic mix. The various ethnic groups would tend to stick with their kind, with areas within the hall considered unofficially reserved for particular groups. However, everyone in the hall was listening and dancing to the same music and buying drinks at the same bar.

Packers Hall was about as simple a building as one could imagine. It was completely open inside except for supporting wood columns and beams that held up a hip roof. A polished hardwood floor lay in the middle of the building, surrounded by a wide border of paving stones. Two large pot-bellied stoves in opposite corners furnished heat and double doors at each end were kept open in the summer to cool it down. There was a bar on one side and a raised platform for musicians on the other. Benches and tables filled the remaining space around the edges of the dance floor.

It was after eight o'clock when the three young meat cutters arrived. Tickets cost ten cents. The back of their hand was stamped with a black ink marker to show they had paid. Things were moving at a lively pace. A Bohemian band was playing a polka and dancers were flying around the floor.

Heinrich saw Maria and her friends sitting at a table.

Emil warned, "Don't go over there, that's Bohunk territory."

Heinrich started moving in that direction. "That one with the curly hair, cute as hell."

"Your eyes getting bad? She has a horse face!"

"Look at those tits."

"I have to give you that."

Bohemian and Polish men stood along the wall in back of the tables watching the advance of the three encroachers.

Maria seemed a little apprehensive as they approached. She forced a smile. "My favorite hog killers, aren't you lost? The Krauts are on the other side of the band."

"How about introducing your friends?" Heinrich asked.

About that time, three big Bohemians moved away from the wall, surrounded the table and asked the girls to dance.

The three young Germans stood by, watching the girls being escorted to the dance floor.

Heinrich looked peeved. "Hell of a way to treat company."

Emil surmised that it was lucky those goons just wanted to dance. "Must not be drunk yet. Anyone thirsty?"

They got a pitcher of beer, then used good judgement and settled at a table on the German side of the bandstand.

After killing the pitcher and fetching another one, they started surveying the situation. The Irish were located directly across the dance floor. A mixture of Americans at least one generation past getting off the boats were on the other side of the floor on the far side of the bar. The Bohemian area included Poles any other eastern Europeans and was located on the other side of the bandstand.

Emil advised, "Anything with a skirt will do."

Heinrich was not so sure. "Can't get my mind off the curly haired one."

"Find a Kraut with big tits. Lots of them around."

Karl figured it was the forbidden fruit that appealed to his friend. "Heinrich wants a challenge."

"He's looking in the right place."

They finished off another pitcher. Heinrich wove through the dancers and got a refill.

"Good thing you can't get drunk on beer," he slurred when he got back.

Emil raised his mug. "I'll drink to that."

Heinrich drained his mug and stood up. "I'm going to dance with ole Curly Hair."

At that particular time, Karl and Emil really weren't caring what Heinrich wanted to do.

They weren't too sure if they were seeing right when Heinrich returned. He had Maria, Curly Hair, and the other girl in tow. Maria was talking, "Not enough men and the ones there are all too drunk." She pointed at the full-busted one. "Margarete," she said, and pointing to the other one, "and Annette."

Heinrich led Margarete to the floor as a waltz began. Emil picked Annette. That left Karl and Maria, an unlikely pair.

"Come on, Karl," Maria motioned towards the floor.

Karl was sober enough to know that he had never danced before. "Can't dance," he explained.

"You can walk. Come on, I'll teach you"

"Your left hand, here, your other hand in the middle of my back, hold me tight," she giggled, "Don't be afraid of me." They started moving on the crowded floor. Maria put her weight into the task, leading while dancing backwards. "Forget what you are doing. Listen to the music, follow me. Mm-mm-mm de hum" she hummed, accentuating the beat of the waltz. Karl picked up the rhythm and with Maria pushing and pulling, felt his body and feet moving in time with the sound.

Maria complimented him, "You're doing real good. Next we do the polka."

"I don't think so."

They continued dancing and drinking until the band shut down at midnight. Heinrich and Margarete were getting along all right, while Emil and Annette were getting along really well.

The men walked the women partway home. There was a mutual agreement that the men need not cross the boundary into the Bohemian part of town.

*       *       *       *

Karl wound up with a large head and a sour beer taste in his mouth the next morning. He checked: he had spent his planned weekly savings plus a lot more.

His resolved to mend his ways, but the following Saturday was a repeat of the previous week. As the summer wore on it became apparent that his plans were seriously in trouble, due only in part to his reduced income.

One Saturday started out particularly warm. Heinrich was complaining that it was even too hot to play penny ante. Karl had an idea. "There is a lake east of here someplace, a big lake."

Heinrich remembered. "I thought it was an ocean."

"Right. How about heading in that direction, see if we can find it?"

"Let's see if Emil wants to go."

They headed east on Thirty-ninth Street, a main east-west street that should take them to the lake. They walked past the stockyards and out of the neighborhood where they had pretty much confined themselves since taking their slaughterhouse jobs.

One thing they noticed as they moved away from the packing house neighborhood was that the air was becoming different. Heinrich was the first to comment on it.

"What's that I smell?"

They all sniffed the air. Karl figured it out.

"That's fresh air."

They had become so accustomed to the foul odors of the packing house neighborhood that fresh air smelled foreign to them.

The street they were walking on looked like the street on which they had entered the packing house neighborhood over a year before. Some gravel but mostly dirt with ruts still visible from wetter days. There was a lot of construction going on, and like most streets in Chicago, it was straight and flat.

The sun was beating down. After they had walked a couple of miles on Thirty-ninth Street, sweat was starting to create designs on their shirts. There were no signs of a lake as far as they could see.

"Are you sure there is a lake?" Emil asked.

Heinrich assured him that he had seen it when they came into Chicago, and it was a big one.

After a while they began seeing large houses with large yards and manicured lawns. Soon after that they ran into a town square with a few shops and a saloon. Just beyond that was a rail track that ran parallel to a lake. It was a big lake, much as Karl had described.

They crossed the tracks and approached the lake, which appeared to be bordered by large boulders, but with pockets of sandy beach dispersed among them at the water's edge. The area seemed deserted except for four young boys in the buff jumping off a large rock in the water a city block up the shore from where the exploring meat packing plant workers stood.

Heinrich observed that the kids had the right idea and was soon shedding his clothes. Karl and Emil followed suit. The water was deliciously cool. They splashed in the water like little kids, blew bubbles, and tried dog paddling in the deeper water.

After a time they became aware of company, three girls, young women really, standing on the beach near where their clothes were piled. They were wearing short, belted dresses with full length sleeves over a kind of blowsy bloomers tied at the ankles. They wore sun bonnets and sandals. The men were able to observe these details while standing waist deep in the lake. The women were talking and observing the men.

The three men recognized that they had a problem of some kind.

Heinrich offered a solution. "I'll just walk out and they will scatter like scared chickens."

Karl wasn't sure that was a good idea. "Let's think about that."

Emil agreed. "Maybe we don't want to scare them."

Karl agreed with Emil and told Heinrich, "Ask them if they will throw our clothes to us."

Heinrich raised his voice so it would carry to where the girls were guarding the clothes.

"Vould you please throw us da clothes?" His heavy accent clearly identified his foreign origin.

"These your clothes?" one called out.

"Ya."

Some discussion ensued.

One of the women sorted through the pile of clothes, threw in one pair of pants, then the other two pairs.

The men sensed they had gotten all they were going to get, retrieved the pants and pulled them on under the water. Then they walked out to claim their shirts.

The women stood around and watched the men finish dressing.

The three women appeared to all be about the same age, twenty, plus or minus a couple of years. They introduced themselves as Angela, Mary, and Kathryn, and said they lived in some of the big houses nearby. They were home for the summer after attending school back east.

Karl noticed they talked differently than most people he knew. Like real Americans. He supposed the women thought the three men talked funny.

What did the men do?

Heinrich answered, "Work for the railroad, firemen, working to be engineers."

Karl and Emil hid their surprise at the sudden career change.

Heinrich continued, "We were going to get a couple of bottles of beer at the saloon and have a picnic. Care to join us?"

"What do you have to eat?"

"Not that kind of picnic."

"We would prefer wine, white wine."

"No problem."

Karl and Emil were being carried along by their friend's extemporaneous plans, but they weren't complaining.

It was decided. Karl and Heinrich would get the supplies, and Emil would stay at the beach with the women.

While on their mission, Karl wanted to know how they would pay for this picnic.

"I have my week's pay in my pocket," Heinrich replied, "You and Emil can owe me."

Three quarts of beer, three liters of white wine and a deposit on six tin cups just about wiped out Heinrich's week's pay. Karl considered it a risky investment.

They alternated between wading in the cool water, lying on the warm sand, drinking beer and wine, and becoming better acquainted. The women seemed to find the young men amusing, their accents cute. The men learned that the outfits the women were wearing represented the latest styles in swim wear.

The afternoon wore on and the picnickers mellowed as the beer and wine got used up. The group started to shift into a one-on-one arrangement. Karl found himself talking mostly to Mary.

Her head was crowned by a mass of curly brown hair and she had a strong lithe figure. Her name was Mary Shaffer and she was a third-generation German American.

"My grandfather was of Prussian stock too. He farmed in Pennsylvania. Are you really railroad men?"

"Sure."

"Your clothes kind of smell like animals."

"Oh, we have been running trains into the stockyards. It rubs off."

"It certainly does."

The sun was turning a dull red as it settled towards the horizon. The beer and wine was used up, so they decided to explore the shoreline for a while. They straggled along the beach in couples, climbing up and over rocks, wading in and out of the water. Karl and Mary lagged behind, then waded out to where the water was up to Karl's chest. Mary, being shorter, was hanging onto him and bobbing like a cork. Karl put his hands on Mary's waist. The short skirt had floated upward and he felt her bare skin at the top of her bloomer bottoms. He discovered Mary was not wearing anything under the bloomers. He pushed the bloomers down. Mary did not resist and he stroked the pubic hair between her legs.

The other couples returned. It was time to start back. The men walked the women back to the town square. They would find their own way from there.

The three men recapped the afternoon's events on the long walk to the Back of the Yards.

Karl was reflective. "We live in different worlds."

Emil asked, "Who does?"

"Them women and us."

"Ya," Heinrich agreed, "but they are people just like us, different situation, but still people like us. They get hot between the legs just like peasant girls."

Emil laughed. "That is one way to think of it."

Heinrich figured it was a better way to spend an afternoon than playing penny ante at O'Riley's, but more expensive.

Emil remembered that they were missing the Saturday night dance.

Karl spoke up, "And your Annette."

"Ya, my Annette."

Heinrich was still seeing Margarete at the dances. That was the extent of it. Emil and Annette were a different matter. Whenever possible, they were together. This had started to attract the scrutiny of Annette's family, who weren't sure they approved.

The discovery of the lake provided an alternative to the Back of the Yard saloons for the remainder of the summer. They took the long walk almost every weekend, sometimes on Saturday, sometimes on Sunday. It improved Karl's outlook. He was not making more money, but was spending less, and he felt better about himself. Unfortunately, they never ran into the young women that lived in the big houses again.

Finally, cooler fall weather and increased activity at the plant terminated the beach sojourns. They were running six twelve-hour days again and Karl was again saving money at the planned rate. The summer had been a disaster financially. Karl was lucky to have broken even, considering the reduced days and spending more than he should have. Hopefully he would be able to make it up during the coming winter. Maybe he could still be out of there in two years.

# CHAPTER 13

▼

# A SETBACK

The day had not started out well. Karl's stomach was upset and he was not able to eat his normal large breakfast. Nothing to worry about, it was not unusual to get sick once or twice a year. Sickness had never prevented Karl from working. He would just work the sickness out. However, as the day progressed, it didn't get better, it got worse. By the middle of the afternoon, he was feeling weak. He would sweat profusely and then become chilled. His whole body ached. He was going on sheer will power and it was not enough. He was falling behind. The energy he needed just was not there, and Dan soon noticed that he was lagging.

"Karl, get the lead out. Keep up with the line."

Karl braced himself, grabbed onto the next carcass coming down the line, then suddenly felt himself losing his balance. He couldn't stop from falling back against a wall and then crumbling to the floor.

Dan was yelling, "Tighten up the line, Pete, Nick, pick up Karl's work. Keep it going, pick up the pace."

Then he walked over to where Karl lay, took him by the shoulders, and raised him to a sitting position.

By then Karl had revived and opened his eyes. It took him a moment to figure out what happened. He saw Dan looking at him with a worried expression on his face. "Can't do it, don't know what's wrong."

Dan appeared relieved to see he had come to. "Get yourself home if you can. I'll mark you down for the day so you get paid." Then he straightened up and went back to work.

Karl staggered back to the apartment. He fell into bed and spent the night in a sick daze, alternately sweating and freezing. He became delusional, his mind played tricks on itself, and he would wake up screaming.

Heinrich made himself up a bed on the floor, giving Karl space to work out the demons in his body. He hoped that he wouldn't become infected with whatever Karl had.

The next morning when it was time to go to work, Karl was awake, but shivering, despite piling on every blanket and all the clothes he had. He would not be going to work.

As Heinrich worked his shift, he thought about Karl, hoping he was all right and wondering if he should try to get a doctor. He decided against the doctor. It would cost money Karl probably would not want to spend, and it most likely would do no good. Karl's only defense was a strong young body that would have to overcome whatever had him in its hold.

When Heinrich returned that evening, Karl was still in bed, sleeping fitfully, with most of his blankets thrown off. Heinrich felt Karl's forehead. It was burning hot.

The next day when Heinrich went to work, someone had taken Karl's place on the line.

Karl lost track of time. Sometimes it was daylight when he woke, sometimes it was dark. He was not sure what day or night it was. He had vivid dreams, some about his home in Prussia and his mother who used to comfort him when he was ill. Now she could only provide comfort in his dreams.

A week after Karl came down with his illness, Heinrich had his worst fear realized. He was coming down with a sickness, most likely the same thing that had almost completely immobilized Karl. It came over him while he was at work. It was all he could do to make it through the end of the day, drag himself to the apartment, and fall into his temporary bed. The next morning he was feverish. He knew he could not walk the half mile to work, much less do his job on the line.

Karl began to recover about the time Heinrich was getting sick. Karl was acutely sympathetic to Heinrich's condition, but as in his own case, could do little to help his friend.

Though feeling better, Karl was still extremely weak. He had lost a lot of weight from a body that had little to spare. During the first few days of his recovery, he was hardly strong enough to prepare himself meals, something he knew he had to do to get back his strength.

While it seemed clear that Heinrich suffered from the same illness as Karl, it did not strike him nearly as severely. Within two days, Heinrich's illness was abating. He was recovering at pace with Karl and maybe even faster.

However, as far as work was concerned, the effect was the same. They had both been replaced on the line and were now unemployed. Both of them went back to talk to Dan and both were told the same thing. They had been permanently replaced, and there was nothing Dan could do to help them.

When Karl and Heinrich had started, the plant was hiring a lot of people and tried to fit anyone in that looked like they could do the work. But now they were fully staffed and were only looking for replacements. Replacements for people who became ill, like they had, or who left for other reasons. There was a hiring hall where job seekers gathered at six a.m. every morning, hopeful that there would be an opening and they would be selected.

Now they were two among many seeking work, hoping that the company man selecting workers would pick them out of the crowd for any of the available openings. Their one-and-a-half year's experience had little value. Anyone fresh off the boat could do their job after a few hours of training. Their only hope was that they would appear strong and healthy and catch the eye of the hiring clerk when the need for help occurred.

Karl was not a large man. He had never carried a lot of weight on his sparse frame, and after two weeks of sickness and recovery, he looked anemic compared to most of the other men in the hall.

Heinrich was huskier. Having been less ill, he made a better showing than Karl, but there were a lot of large, strong young men in that hall. The larger men were more visible, and it was easy to assume that larger meant stronger and more able to work hard during the long twelve-hour shifts.

After two weeks of going to the hiring hall every morning, and after having been passed over many times when jobs became available, Heinrich and Karl were becoming concerned.

There was no money coming in but they still had expenses. They were now living off their savings. Karl had accumulated over one hundred dollars before he became ill. Heinrich had not saved as much, but inspired by Karl's example, did have twenty-five dollars put away. They were not in immediate danger of being put out into the street or of having to beg for food. But for Karl, taking money out of his savings was painful.

Karl knew that just being in America would not guarantee one of success. He was learning now that working hard and diligently in America was no guarantor of success either. He found himself having serious doubts about his plan to homestead land. Would he be trapped in a dead- end job, working hard to just have enough to eat and a place to sleep? In the short term that was certainly the case. He needed some income now just to survive, never mind saving for his dream.

He confided to Heinrich, "Looks like I'll have to do nigger work again to keep my head above water."

Heinrich wasn't so sure of that description anymore. "I've seen some of them at the plant, and I'll bet they get paid the same as you and me."

"Why not? You should get paid for what you do, not what you look like. Anyway, whatever you call it, I have to do some kind of work that will pay for the groceries or I'll be using up all my savings."

There were still jobs that no one else wanted, mostly because they paid so little a person couldn't afford to work them, and Karl took one of those. He got seventy-five cents a day, bussing in a saloon, working from ten in the morning until ten at night. It was much like the job Heinrich had been doing in Baltimore.

The job allowed Karl to be in the hiring hall at six a.m., in case there were any jobs at the packing plant and it paid enough to cover his part of their living expenses.

\*    \*    \*    \*

Despite their dire financial situation, they tried to make it to Flanagan's at least once a week, on Sunday afternoons now since Karl worked Saturday nights.

Emil usually joined them. He and Annette were still tight as two ticks in winter. Heinrich and Margarete hadn't seen each other since Heinrich got sick. Maria said Margarete was seeing some big Bohemian.

One Sunday Emil started off with, "Got a problem."

"So, who doesn't?" Karl wanted to know. "At least you still got a job on the line."

"A big problem."

"Ya, tell us."

"Annette is expecting."

Karl and Heinrich were stopped cold for a moment. This was big problem.

"How did you manage that?" Karl finally asked. "Her family is watching all the time."

"Not quite."

"I'll bet her Pa's old flint lock is loaded and ready."

Heinrich wanted to know when the wedding was going to be.

"It might have happened already, but there are a couple of things holding it up. For one thing, you know I'm German, and you know Annette is Bohemian. Bohemians marry Bohemians."

Heinrich agreed, "Ya, but you have this situation."

"That's right, there is no way that can be changed."

"The other problem is kinda the same. Annette is Catholic, and Catholics can only marry Catholics, and I'm not."

Karl was sympathetic. "Big problem alright."

Heinrich looked at it more positively. "Sounds like you have an out."

"I really want to marry her."

Maria bustled up about that time. "Heinrich, didn't see you at the dance."

"Maybe that's because I wasn't there."

"Saw Emil."

"We were just talking about that."

"Well, he better get the lead out."

"He can't. The Pope won't marry them and he isn't Bohemian."

"He has to convert, that's all."

"How can a German become a Bohemian?"

"Never thought about that part of it."

"Why don't you get us a pitcher of beer? Hard to think."

The situation could not be ignored or delayed indefinitely. Another week went by and a solution was finally worked out. There was some give and take, and a compromise of sorts.

Annette's family swallowed hard, and allowed that as Emil was from Bavaria, very near to Bohemia, that under the circumstances it probably was close enough.

The church problem was resolved by some give on Emil's part. Emil would convert on paper, but it was understood by the family that you could lead a horse to the tank, but you might not be able to make it drink.

They would be married right after New Year's.

Once all the issues were settled, the family went all out in planning the wedding. The first daughter to be married in America, even under trying circumstances, was going to have a wedding in the best Bohemian tradition. Fortunately, it was a large family, all of whom were assessed, and some of the vendors extended credit, making the whole thing financially feasible.

Packers Hall would be the location of the reception. A four-piece polka band was hired and enough food and drinks to satisfy a good-sized village were procured. When the whole Bohemian community was included, this came to about the same thing.

The guests on the groom's side were limited by several factors. Emil did not have any immediate relatives anywhere near Chicago, and the German community, though large, was not as cohesive as its Bohemian counterpart. This was probably a good thing because the two ethnic groups didn't mix well, and an affair where there would be liquor in many forms might not be a good time to test that relationship. In addition to Heinrich who was best man and Karl who was also part of the wedding party, Emil had invited half a dozen men who worked on the line with him. Two of them were Irish and the rest were Germans.

The wedding date came up soon enough. It was on the first Saturday after New Year's Day. Karl took the day off from his job at the saloon. The wedding ceremony was at the Catholic church at eight p.m. and lasted less than a half hour. In consideration of the circumstances; as well as the groom's tepid adherence to the Catholic faith, the ceremony was the simplest and shortest in the church's repertoire. It was after the church ceremony and in the rented hall that the real wedding celebration took shape. The bride and groom danced the first dance, a signal for the dancing, drinking, and eating to proceed.

Karl danced a ritual dance with the bride.

Annette was radiant, only protruding a little in front.

Karl asked if she had any idea last summer that she would be marrying one of those men she met at the Packers Hall.

She laughed. "It took a while for Emil to figure it out, longer than it took me."

The party quickly gained momentum. The band was playing almost continuously and the dance floor was crowded. Karl had to wonder at how these men, who spent their days on the killing floor, turned into nimble dancers on Saturday nights. During the fast polkas the couples whirled like dervishes, and during a traditional waltz, the real dancers would emerge, sweeping about the floor as if they were in an aristocrat's ballroom. Margarete was there, dancing with a really big fellow. He must be the Bohemian friend Maria had talked about.

Drinks were flowing freely and some people seemed to be set on drinking as much as possible before the supply dried up. Karl and Heinrich took a break to sample a tapped keg of beer. Heinrich saw Margarete standing with some of her friends.

"I think I should ask Margarete for a dance."

Karl cautioned him. "Did you see the size of her friend?"

"All I'm going to do is dance with her."

"That's for sure."

Emil was mixing with the crowd and stopped to talk to Karl. They watched Heinrich and Margarete circle the floor. As the twirling couple approached them, Margarete's big friend emerged from the crowd, got behind Heinrich, and without introducing himself, grabbed him around the waist, lifted him up and threw him towards where Emil and Karl were standing. He landed right at their feet.

Karl encouraged Heinrich. "Go fight the man. Show him what is what." But before Heinrich could act, circumstances saved him. Apparently there was some bad blood between another big Bohunk and Margarete's friend, and he used the opportunity to join in. The two big men were soon rolling on the floor.

"Damn," Karl observed, "that big fellow is spoiling your chance to get even."

As the night wore on, the revelry kept going, but at a slower pace. The band, which had been playing with zest, was now taking long breaks. Men were lying in the corners and along the wall, sleeping or passed out. Another one was under the food table.

But nobody wanted the party or the night to end. This was such a rare event in their otherwise drab lives that they did not want to give it up. They clung to it, making it last as long as they could.

# CHAPTER 14

▼

# TIME FOR A CHANGE

At the time of the wedding, Karl and Heinrich's fortunes were at a low ebb. Maybe the wedding was a harbinger of better times. Soon after the wedding Heinrich caught the eye of the hiring clerk, and he was hired to work in a cutting line. It wasn't Dan's line, but one like it.

Karl was getting very anxious and concerned. Would he ever get a job in the packing plant again? Karl was not enthralled with packing plant work, but it was the means he was counting on to get to his planned goal.

One morning Karl met a person in the hiring hall that he knew from the old cutting line. Joe Kosovich. He left his job to meet a bride that had come over from the old country. He met her when she landed in New York City. He had been gone two weeks and this was the first day in the hall. He was picked right away to work in the big cooler. A choice job. Karl was flabbergasted. There was nothing outstanding about this fellow. He was about the same size and weight as Karl.

Karl exclaimed, "I have been in this hiring hall for months. You come in and get a job the first day.

Joe put his arm around Karl's shoulder, "There is something you should know Karl. Come by the hall in the afternoon. The hiring clerk will be here. If you happen to leave an envelope with two dollars in it, it will make a big difference the next morning."

Karl followed Joe's suggestion, took a break from his saloon job that afternoon and stopped by the hiring hall. The hiring clerk was there. He was a little man, not over five feet tall, and didn't carry an ounce of fat. His head was disproportionately large, with a hook nose and a wisp of grey hair. His face was clean shaven. He had worn the same black pants and coat every day that Karl had come to the hiring hall. The white shirt had been changed occasionally.

Karl handed a white, unsealed envelope containing the two dollars to the clerk. The clerk took a quick glance at the envelope's contents, then looked Karl over carefully.

He instructed Karl, "Stand along the wall to my right in the morning." He put the envelope in a drawer.

Karl, not knowing quite what to do at that point, stood staring at the clerk.

The clerk impatiently drummed his fingers on the desk for a moment, then spoke. "Goodby. Have a good day, young man."

The next morning Karl was selected. "Got a job on the hog killing floor for you, report in the morning at six a.m."

Karl knew the killing floor, and it would not have been his first choice of jobs. Although he was familiar with the killing floor and knew what to expect, it was still a shock to his system when he was first fully exposed to it. It was work that necessitated that his body and mind acquire a detachment from the effort involved.

The animals were driven up a long ramp to near the top of the plant, where workers attached a bar to one of the rear legs of each animal and hooked it to a wheel twelve feet in diameter. The wheel carried the animals up and over to a track from which they would be hanging chest high off the floor, squealing loudly. As they came onto the track, Karl and fellow workers cut their throats. The blood would gush out, driven by the pressure built up by the frantic muscular action during the hog's final moments. They tried to catch the blood in holding tanks, but a portion always escaped. As a result the workers stood in an inch or more of blood all day and despite the heavy leather aprons they wore, their clothes were soon soaked. The human psyche is adaptable, and Karl's system did adjust to the hellish environment; nevertheless he hated the work, and endured it only because he believed it would enable him to reach the goal he had set for himself.

After getting back to working full time, Karl reviewed his finances, and was not pleased with the progress he was making. He had been falling short of his goal of saving ten dollars a month even before the slow summer and his sickness demolished his plan to be out of Chicago in two years. He counted his savings;

Seventy nine dollars and twenty cents. He would not be ready to leave for a long time at the rate he was going.

Hot summer days were soon upon them again, and with them came shortened work weeks. This summer Karl was expecting the curtailed schedule, so when it happened, he was able to adjust without the difficulties of the previous summer. He did not save much, but was able to budget his expenses better.

He didn't avoid the saloons completely, but they didn't take over his life either. Walking to the lake was a diversion he and Heinrich savored on hot week-end days, and he started exploring other directions as well, sometimes walking towards downtown, or west out into the countryside.

One Saturday night that summer they made one of their regular stops at Flanagan's.

Maria sauntered over. "I think I smell some slaughterhouse men."

"Your favorite kind?" Heinrich asked.

Maria shrugged, "If there's no other choice."

"What have you got against us anyway?"

"Maybe if you took a bath, once in a while…?"

Heinrich was defensive. "Hell, I did—once."

"What can I get you fellows?"

"The usual. Pitcher of beer, two mugs."

Maria was back with the beer. "See much of Emil?"

"Still cutting on the line. He's pretty tied down now."

"When are you boys getting married?"

"Are you available?"

"Sure, are you proposing?"

"Good luck. Bring another mug, here comes Isadore."

They were joined by Isadore the Swede, the person who had replaced Emil at the Flanagan's get-togethers.

"Isadore, so what the hell is happening with you? Still shoveling guts?" Heinrich asked as he filled three glasses.

"Hell no, got promoted, shoveling pig shit now. Takes more know-how than being a cutter, that's for sure."

"Have you reached your goal, or are you thinking of going even higher?"

"I think I have peaked in this business, so I'm thinking of moving to another line of work."

"Ya, what?"

"Well, I might go back to what I was doing before I came here. You know how things always look better on the other side of the fence. I was lumber jacking up in Wisconsin, spent five months up in the woods last winter with sixty dirty men in a logging camp. Nothing to do but work twelve hours a day. After a while you start wondering if there might be a better way to be spending your time. But now I'm looking at it from a different way. When you were working out in the woods in the cold winter air, it was clean, didn't smell like this place, and you had a partner on the other end of the saw and as long as you cut your share of trees, nobody bothered you. And you worked every day except Christmas and Sundays. No off days, no short days. A bunk house with sixty smelly men might not seem like real fun, but everybody got along, and we didn't go hungry. They pay you cash when you finish."

The word, "cash," piqued Karl's interest. His savings had been close to a standstill this past year, the total was still only a little over a hundred dollars. After over two years at the job, he was hardly holding his own. He could spend the rest of his life trying to get a stake at this rate.

"How much cash you talking about?."

"An ordinary lumber jack should have over a hundred dollars in his pocket in the spring.

Do you think they would take anyone besides dumb Swedes?" Karl asked.

"I don't know. Taking Germans might be pushing it, but if you are crazy enough to go out in the woods and cut trees when it is thirty degrees below, they might take you."

"For over a hundred dollars in my pocket, I might be. When do you go into the woods?"

"We usually go in November. Come out, March, April."

"That's three months away."

"Well, they start lining up the crews about this time for the next year."

"What do you have to do to be a lumberjack?"

"Well, you have to have some warm clothes, an axe, and a good attitude."

"An axe?"

"Ya, they furnish all the tools except an axe, but you can get that at the camp store, put it on the books. Then it's yours and you have to keep it sharpened, and keep a tight hold on it because everybody is looking for an axe."

They went over the clothes Karl would need and how much everything would cost. Isadore thought he could get most of what was needed second-hand for around ten to fifteen dollars.

"Where are these Wisconsin woods and how much does it cost to get there?"

"The camp is north of a town called Eau Claire. Take a train from Chicago, cost three dollars the last time I rode it."

The idea began sounding better to Karl all the time. He was just staying afloat in the meat packing business, a line of work he never liked. This might be an improvement.

Heinrich had been listening to the conversation with growing interest. He might not be as dumb as some other people he knew, but like Karl he had just about had his fill of what they were doing and was ready to try something different.

Isadore agreed to find out if there would be room for all three of them at the logging camp where he had a contact.

Three weeks later, Isadore let them know that the camp he was going to would have room for a couple of green Germans, so preparations were started to make the trek into the northern woods. They shopped for the warm cloths Isadore said they would need. On the list were two pair of wool pants, shirts and longjohns, a flannel-lined canvas or jean jacket, a fleece-lined overcoat, three pair of wool socks, two pair of canvas gloves, and a pair of mittens with a wool liner. They also needed wool cap, a pair of heavy, calf-high boots and a blanket. By careful shopping at second-hand stores, Karl and Heinrich were able to obtain the items each needed for just under twenty dollars. A Duluth pack to carry all their gear cost each of them another two dollars. The early fall passed without incident, and in the middle of November they were ready to depart for Eau Claire, Wisconsin.

Karl counted his money one more time. Taking out what he needed for the trip to Wisconsin and a little extra, he still had a hundred dollars. He took that money, walked into downtown Chicago, went into the biggest, most impressive-looking bank building on LaSalle Street, and deposited the money into a savings account.

Isadore and the two aspiring lumberjacks left Chicago and the meat packing business with no regrets and without a look back.

# CHAPTER 15

▼

# INTO THE NORTH WOODS

The two aspiring lumberjacks and the one seasoned veteran arrived in Eau Claire by train in the middle of November 1874. As they stepped from the train, Karl and Heinrich saw a bustling good-sized town, something beyond what they had anticipated. They had expected to be on the edge, if not in the middle of a northern wilderness. Sawmills lined the river, a business district was filled with stores, saloons, and boarding houses. A residential area was filled with workers' cottages.

Karl and Heinrich also realized they weren't finished traveling when they got off the train and saw the landscape around Eau Claire. There wasn't a tree in sight. Some brush and slash, signs of where tress had been, but no trees.

When questioned Isadore about this, he looked at them like they had just flunked kindergarten. "We aren't there yet. We have to hike up to Chippewa Falls and catch a boat for another thirty miles and then walk another three days before we reach our camp, Flambeau number three."

Karl took note of the distance they had left to travel. "Walk to Chippewa Falls, boat ride, then walk for three days. You didn't mention that before."

"It's my fault, I forgot I was dealing with people who don't know anything. Anyway, you will like the hike. We sleep under the stars, walk twenty miles a day in the clear fresh air. It will get you in shape for cutting down trees." Isadore continued,"We have to get some supplies for the little hike."

Eau Claire was a major staging area for men making ready to journey to the remote camps, so Isadore, Karl, and Heinrich weren't alone when shopping for that final push to the camp.

They were picking up the things they needed at a general grocery and supply store, when an unlikely pair of men came in. One was of average height, had a wiry build and looked as though he had been carved out of granite. He was probably in his late forties or even early fifties. The second was a Negro who looked to be in his thirties and was abnormally large. He was not fat, just large—tall and wide. They were also getting supplies for an overland hike to a camp, and after exchanging greetings and some information it became apparent that they were going to the same camp as Isadore and his two recruits. The man with granite features spoke with a New Englander's twang and introduced himself as Henry Bradford, camp foreman, and the Negro as Steven Johnson, the best cook in the north woods. Henry suggested they join forces and make the trek together. Isador's group was quick to agree since their north woods experience was limited to the one year Isadore had spent in the camps. Without any formal discussion or agreement, Henry assumed the role of group leader, and no one objected. Henry inquired about what provisions Isadore's group was taking for the trek. He suggested that since Steven was carrying a cooking pan and kettle they could take dry rice and beans and reduce the amount of dried meat and bread needed. He added, "You will need mess kits for the beans and rice. The kettle will be used for making tea as well."

Henry also added dried fruit, raisins, and prunes to the menu. "We will carry an extra day's supplies just in case. Weather can be changeable this time of the year."

Henry continued outlining their needs for the trip to the camp. "Each of you have a blanket, I hope. We will carry three extra blankets. It can get cold, middle of November. Two of us will share an extra blanket, except Steven. He gets his own because of his size. I have a hatchet we can use for building lean-to shelters if we need them."

The next day they started their trek to Chippewa Falls, where they would camp overnight. Karl observed that they were walking through a wasteland, more of the treeless landscape they had seen at Eau Claire, with only slash and stumps left as evidence of a forest. Finally he asked Henry, "Where were all the logs coming from that were being milled in Eau Claire?"

Henry filled him in as they walked. "The Chippewa and Eau Claire rivers and all their tributaries drain a large area filled with pine trees. Eau Claire is located just below where all these river systems come together, so you start logs anywhere up those rivers and they will end up in Eau Claire. That is why there is an Eau Claire, the only reason that there is an Eau Claire."

At Chippewa Falls, they camped overnight near a series of large rapids that prevented boats from navigating the river up from Eau Claire. The next day they joined a group planning to take a boat up the Chippewa River. The boat would not be running much longer. Skim ice was already forming on the slow water at night and a freeze-up could happen any day.

The small steam-powered boat was designed to carry ten people but there were twelve lumberjacks with their equipment waiting to board the boat. They loaded the equipment, and then the men went aboard one at a time. The boat sank lower and lower in the water as the men climbed aboard. Steven the cook was the last man to come on board and his added weight caused the boat to settle precariously low in the water. There were only three inches of freeboard remaining.

Steven sat down in a seat next to Heinrich.

Heinrich noted the overloaded conditions, and Steven's size and heft. "There are times when big is not good."

"Ya suh, can be a problem."

"How about a bunk? You must have to curl up like a pretzel."

"Dat's uh problem all right." Then Steven added, "Got dat fixed at da camp. Rebuilt da cook's bunk, added a foot."

"Good idea. Now if you would add a foot to this boat."

Karl was listening but did not feel like taking part in any small talk. He was holding his breath whenever the boat hit any kind of rapids or ripples. The idea of a couple of extra days of walking began to seem more appealing.

Ten miles up the river they approached rapids that would have been a challenge to an empty boat, much less an overloaded one. To the passengers' relief, the boat's helmsman pulled up to the shore and had the passengers walk the rapids. He took the boat and baggage through without mishap.

After proceeding another hour, the boat reached the mouth of a small river, where two passengers disembarked to begin the overland portion of their trip. That added two inches of freeboard, and after two more stops, only Henry and Isador's party was left in the boat.

With his anxiety caused by the overloaded boat relieved, Karl became more observant of his surroundings. As the boat moved up river, it was hardly perceivable that they were moving through one of the Earth's great forests. There was nothing but stumps, piles of slash, and scattered underbrush visible.

Karl was getting impatient with the lack of trees to cut. He spoke to Henry. "Two days and I haven't seen a real tree. Are you sure there are any trees left up here to cut?"

Henry, the veteran from Maine, had been watching the same scenery with little note until Karl spoke.

"Don't worry, there's still trees to cut. The first trees to go are always those near the rivers. They're the easiest ones to get out. The logging camps are moving upstream to smaller tributaries. It's getting harder to get logs out. I started working the woods when I was a teenager in Maine, worked northern New York and lower Michigan for over two decades before I came here, and there have always been trees to cut and there are still trees to cut. We used to talk about the never-ending forest that will last forever. Now I know that isn't so. The northern forests run out in the prairies of western Minnesota. The government and lumbermen know that and how much is left and how fast it's being cut. It won't last more than another generation. Is that bad? I don't know. Sometimes when I look at trees standing straight as a stick and over a hundred feet in the air and sometimes when I walk into a forest of trees like that, I feel like I'm in a sacred place, like a cathedral. That will be gone and no one will experience that feeling again, and that does seem sad to me. But Karl, don't worry, there will be plenty of trees to cut this winter."

Karl was assured by Henry's words, but was curious about the future of all this cut over land they were observing. "What is going to happen to all this land? Is it good for farming?"

Henry made a motion with his arm that seemed to encompass the universe. "This land is good for growing pine trees, birch, and poplar, not much else. It seems that where there are pine forests, the land is not good for farming. The top soil is shallow and the land is often sandy or swampy. Go west, to the prairie. There's good farming land that stretches to the horizon that is waiting to be claimed, and there are no stumps to be cleared."

Karl appreciated the testimonial. "That is what I'm going to do. After a winter of logging I hope to have enough money to do that. But what's going to happen to this land?"

"Don't know. Lumber companies lease it for a dollar fifty an acre, don't want it after the trees are cut."

The boat moved up the Chippewa until it reached the mouth of the Flambeau, where it turned up the tributary. The Flambeau became narrower, shallower and more filled with debris as they proceeded. After an hour the boat could go no further. The five lumberjacks disembarked with their gear. From here on they would be relying on their legs.

It was mid-afternoon, so they would put in a few miles that day and then make camp. There was a logging trail running along the river, and according to the information Henry had, it would lead them directly to their destination. The group followed the trail until dusk when they pitched camp. The landscape since leaving the river was similar to what they had observed from the boat—cut over land, stumps, slash and brush as far as the eye could see.

It looked like it would be a clear night, unseasonably warm. Nice weather for sleeping under the stars.

Steven took on the job of camp cook. He started a fire and soon had a kettle of rice and beans cooking.

"You boys better get used ta eat'n a lot of these," Steven chuckled as he stirred the kettle.

"Is that what we're going to live on this winter?" Heinrich asked.

"You goin' to get a lot of em, but a lot of other things too. This a good eatin' camp. You won't go hungry. Eggs if we have 'em fro breakfus, pancakes, bacon, oatmeal. Noon, we bring the tote wagon out ta where you're workin' and dat's goin' to be beans and fresh baked bread mostly. Supper, dat's where we pile it on. Meat, salt pork or beef, beans for sure, potatoes, bread. Steven continued, "And mos everyday we have pie, apple or currant. If we get any wild game, fish, we cook dat up. It's a good eatin' camp."

Karl was curious. "How did a nigger ever get to be a camp cook? I haven't seen many niggers up this way."

To Karl's surprise, Steven dropped his stirring spoon, walked over, grabbed him by the collar and picked him off his feet.

"Don't say dat word to me agin, hear?"

Karl was startled. "What to hell are you doing?"

"Don't ever say dat word round me agin."

Henry interjected, "The word 'nigger.' Don't use the word nigger around Steven."

"All right, all right! Let me down, for Christ's sake."

Steven relaxed his grip, set Karl down, went back to his pot of rice and beans and resumed stirring.

Karl had been too startled to be angry, but he was becoming disturbed as things settled down. Isadore and Heinrich had also observed the activity with alarm. Actually, these past couple of days were the first close-up experiences any of the three had with a Negro. What they had observed before and what they had heard other people say was that Negroes in America were considered inferior to whites in every way. They weren't slaves anymore, but they were somewhere between whites and where slaves used to be. None of them believed Negroes should be slaves, but they felt they had their place and that place was somewhere below where white folks were. And besides, everyone they had ever known called them niggers—so what was Steven's problem? One thing was clear however. In strength, Steven was not an inferior person.

Karl wouldn't care if someone called him German, Prussian, a Kraut, asshole, or whatever, as long as it wasn't intended to be offensive. It was all in how you said it or meant it, and Karl didn't say the word nigger in order to offend Steven. That seemed obvious. Why should he get so upset?

Karl felt compelled to speak up. "I didn't mean the word to be bad. I don't see any reason for anyone to get upset, besides me. I got picked up by the back of the neck and was held dangling in the air by that big ni…oof. I should be the one who is upset."

Henry responded, "Karl, to Steven, nigger is nasty word, a put down, a nasty way of saying Negro. How about it, Steven?" Henry looked over at Steven still stirring the kettle. "Why don't you like to be called nigger?"

Steven seemed a little perplexed by the question. "Is a bad word, I jus know it, so don't call me dat. You call me what else you want, but don't call me a nigger."

Henry added, "It isn't just Steven, any Negro would be upset if they were called nigger. Maybe it would be like someone calling you a sodomite. You wouldn't like it even if you liked your own kind. It is like any other word, which is nothing until it means something to people who say it and hear it. Nigger is an offensive word, meant to be one by many people who use it, and it is to Negroes who hear it. Because it is meant to be and thought to be a nasty word, it is."

Karl was impressed. "We have a professor out here in the woods."

Isadore didn't need any further explanation. "Whatever the reason, I'm not going to make the camp cook mad."

Heinrich agreed. "I'll just take your word for it. Steven, I'll never call you nigger, even if tortured."

The unexpected reaction by Steven and the subsequent discussion left everyone a little on edge. They had not solved the world's bigotry problems, but they at least had a better understanding of the sensibilities of the people in their group, and at that level, they could get along, and maybe even get to like each other, regardless of their ancestry, strange quirks, or naivete. The problem was put behind them and they gathered around the fire to eat their evening meal.

"Pass the beans," Heinrich called as he trimmed off a piece of summer sausage with his knife. "Tell you one thing, it smells a lot better here than it did living by the stockyards. And look at those stars. I didn't know there were so many stars."

Steven cleaned out his cooking kettle, then made some tea which they used to wash down the dried fruit they ate for a desert.

Isadore burped appreciatively. "Now bring on the dancing girls."

Heinrich laughed. "No dancing girls for you until next spring."

The moon peaked over the horizon, the fire began to die down and they kicked dead branches and debris out of the way to make room to spread their blankets. The ground was covered with a thick layer of dead pine needles that provided a soft bed for sleeping. They wrapped themselves snugly in their blankets and were soon fast asleep.

They rose early the next day and revived the fire to make some hot tea. They sweetened the tea with honey that Steven had packed and ate hardtack and dried fruit for breakfast.

There was no wind as they set off down the trail. The air felt heavy, damp, and warm for the third week in November. Henry took the lead and set a brisk pace. He felt there was something ominous about the weather.

At mid-afternoon, a solid bank of clouds appeared on the northwestern horizon and were soon filling the sky. A smattering of rain mixed with sleet began to fall. They weren't prepared for rain and were relieved when it turned to all snow. The snow was falling thick, and heavy and a strong wind began to blow from the north, accompanied by a rapidly falling temperature. Henry stopped the column. "Time to put on some warmer clothes," he ordered. They dug out the heavy clothes. They put on their heavy coats and mittens and wrapped scarfs around their throats. The velocity of the wind was steadily increasing, and visibility had rapidly decreased down to two or three feet. The weather had reached a point where the prudent thing to do would be to hunker down, put together as good a shelter as possible, and ride it out where they were. However, Henry was sure he had seen the edge of the uncut forest in the distance before the visibility dropped to near zero. If they could make that, they would be out of the brutal wind. It was worth a try. Henry yelled his intentions to the men, "The standing woods are not far away. We can make it but have to stick together." A lot of tree branches lay in the slash under their feet. "Grab branches, we'll use them to keep us together. Steven, you take the lead." Henry handed Steven a compass, "Head straight north."

They pulled four branches out of the underbrush. Henry shouted further instructions, "Steven is in the lead, I'll take up the rear, the rest of you are in the middle holding onto branches. Anyone lets loose, everyone stops."

No one questioned Henry's instructions. It was not a good time for a debate. Steven headed off through the slash like a determined ox. He broke a path through the slash, rounding stumps and brush piles, always returning to a due north heading. Occasionally he would stop. They would cluster together to be sure all five were accounted for. Steven would squint at the compass to assure himself of the needle's direction and set off again.

Karl was becoming exhausted. Just breathing was an effort in this wind, and stumbling through the brush with the snow starting to pile up was taxing his body. The driving snow stung his face and he drew his scarf up, covering all of his face except a slit large enough to see. He was right behind Steven who kept plunging ahead, breaking the trail. Steven was only three or four feet ahead of Karl, but at times he was obliterated by the flying snow. Even though Steven was breaking the trail for him to follow, Karl was struggling to keep up. He was developing an appreciation for the strength of the man leading them.

Isadore fell, tripped by a branch, and the line of men came to a stop. Isadore regained his footing, and Steven, assured that everyone was still with him, set off on a north heading again.

A dark wall loomed up in front of them and suddenly they were in the standing forest. They continued on until the effect of the wind was dampened by the trees. The wind still roared through the treetops, but the velocity on the ground was reduced dramatically. Only occasional whirls of wind found their way through the forest canopy.

Steven stopped, not sure what to do at that point. The men gathered together. They were so bundled up that it was hard to recognize one from the other.

Henry looked around. "We are out of the wind, but we need to find some protection from falling trees. We need to find some dead falls, set up camp among them. Keep heading north until we find a good spot."

Steven led again, breaking a trail until they found a spot where previously fallen trees provided the protection that Henry was looking for. They built two lean-to shelters covered with pine boughs and started a fire near open ends of the shelters. They covered the lean-to floors with more pine boughs. While the construction was going on, Steven heated up some beans and supplemented them with hardtack, dried meat and fruit. They kept the fire burning all night and were quite comfortable.

The next morning the storm continued at a lower intensity, and the temperature had dropped dramatically. However, because the forest was protecting them from the wind, Henry pronounced that conditions were fit for traveling. They would get underway as soon as they had breakfast.

Travel would be difficult because of the deep snow and the bitter cold. Steven, the strong one, would again break a trail.

Karl and Heinrich were pleased to learn that sub-zero temperatures would not freeze them in their tracks, and for that matter, they found themselves getting so warm from the hard physical effort needed to move through the snow that they had to remove some of their clothing.

They proceeded steadily, though slowly because of the deep snow, and as a result had to camp out two more nights. The extra night on the trail did not pose a problem since Henry had insisted they carry extra supplies for such a possibility.

# CHAPTER 16

▼

# LOGGING CAMP

They arrived at the camp around noon. Three buildings made of logs sat among some scattered pine trees. There were two very long narrow buildings, each about a 150 feet long. One of the long buildings was approximately thirty feet wide, the other building was narrower at about twenty feet. The third smaller building was about twenty feet square.

Henry told them they should spend the rest of the day getting settled. "Tomorrow you will go into the woods with some veterans to get acquainted with the work. Not a lot to learn, mostly getting your body trained to saw and chop. That will come soon enough. Learn something about being careful. This is dangerous work. In a couple of weeks you will be expected to be cutting with the best of them."

They entered the larger of the two long buildings. On the right side of the entryway was a partitioned-off area. Steven paused, walked over to the open end and peered in, "Dis looks good," he remarked. "Good thing, dis camp is a long ways from anywhere. Won't be makin' many tote runs back to Eau Claire."

The others looked in and could see a lot of shelves and bins stocked with all kinds of food commodities. There were sacks of beans, sugar, salt; flour, rolled oats, coffee beans, and rice. Wheels of cheese were stacked on shelves, salted pork in barrels; hanging slabs of bacon, dried beef; pails of honey, dried prunes, currants, raisins, and apples.

"That's the dingle, sort of a big pantry," Isadore explained. "They store stuff in there that don't care if it freezes."

Henry told them he had to get to his job as camp foreman. He needed to find out who had made it to camp so far. He headed into a small room across the hall from the dingle. That would serve as his bunk room as well as the office he would share with the camp clerk.

Steven said it was time for him to get to work also. He headed through the door to the right of the entryway that led into the cook shanty.

To the left of the entryway was another partitioned off area where there was a counter and a bunch of shelves with clothing, other goods. Karl asked, "Is that where I get my axe?"

"That's the wanigan," Isadore answered. "You can buy clothes, tobacco, and an axe. They keep a tab, deduct it from your pay in the spring."

"Dingle, wanigan, what kind of language is that?" Heinrich asked. "I've got enough trouble with English. And what the hell is a tote?"

Isadore laughed. "We'll have you talking lumberjack soon enough. A tote is something you haul stuff in. In the winter it is a wagon box on sled runners."

There was another door across the hall from the wanigan. Isadore pointed to it. "That's the file room. The file man works in there, sharpens a saw for you everyday. You turn your saw in there at the end of the day and pick up a sharp one in the morning."

To the left of the entryway was the bunk house. Isadore lead the group into it. "Pick out any bunk that don't have a blanket or gear on it. Throw your gear on it and it's yours for the rest of the winter." The empty beds had puffed up burlap bags laying on them and Karl could tell by the feel and smell that the filling was pine boughs.

Isadore confirmed his discovery. "Sleep good, but a lot of small varmints come to life when it warms up. Those jiggers can drive you crazy. Some men even take baths and wash their clothes in the middle of the winter. Don't help much from what I can tell."

The bunk room had seven two-level bunks along each side of the room. With two men sleeping on each level there were accommodations for fifty-six men.

Isadore suggested that they pick something along the left wall. That, he explained, was sort of the German area. "Birds of a feather flock together."

"Even in the woods."

"Ya, even in the woods."

Karl and Heinrich decided to share a top bunk near a big stove at the near end of the room. They were thinking warm—higher up and near one of the stoves.

There were two wood burning stoves, one at the far end and one at the near end of the room.

The room's furniture, besides the bunks, consisted of deacon's benches made of split logs that ran along the ends of the bunks, three tables about half normal height, and a dozen stumps that could be used as chairs were scattered about the room. There were half a dozen spittoons placed around the room, although it appeared that they could use more. Kerosene lamps hanging from the ceiling furnished lighting. In the center of the room between the two stoves was a grinding wheel. Isadore pointed to it, "That is where you sharpen your axe."

At the far end of the bunkhouse was a long dry sink where three soap dishes, and three wash pans sat. Two roll towels and a mirror were hung on the wall in back of the dry sink. There was also a strop for sharpening razors hanging on the wall.

Isadore filled them in on bunk living. "Fifty sweaty lumberjacks eating a lot of beans, smelly clothes drying, tobacco smoke. It can get pretty ripe at times."

"Bad as the stockyards?"

"Not that bad. Come on, I'll show you the rest of the camp."

The other long log building was the barn where the camp horses and oxen were kept when they weren't working. Hay was stacked near one end of the barn and one of the stalls served as a place to store grain for the animals. There were stalls along one side with room for a passageway behind them. Harnesses were hung from pegs on the posts that divided the stalls, and heavy chains used for the oxen were draped over logs ranged along the passageway wall. The barn's floor was made of split logs.

Most of the animals were in their stalls, resting and eating hay. Soon the work would start and there would be few animals lounging in the barn during the day. Some of the teamsters were cleaning the stalls and putting down fresh bedding. The building looked clean and cozy and had an earthy smell that reminded Karl of the Hohenzollern estate horse barn in Prussia.

"Why so many animals?" Karl asked.

"To get the logs to the river," Isadore explained. "That's a big part of the work. Most teamsters are farmers, bring their horses and oxen here in the winter to make a little extra money. A teamster with a team of horses can make two dollars a day. Twice as much as lumberjacks like us."

The smaller building was a blacksmith shop and tool shed. A penetrating smell of burning coke, wood, and hot iron filled the air. An iron bar was laying in the red-hot coals and a large man in shirt sleeves was maneuvering the bar with some tongs. He wore a leather apron, and streaks of grey in his beard indicated that he was older than most of the men in camp.

The man drew the white-hot bar out of the forge and laid it on an anvil. Sparks flew as he pounded the iron into a hook-shaped object. The iron turned grey and he pushed it back into the red-hot coals, then acknowledged the curious men watching him.

Isadore introduced him, "Johann, blacksmith, jack-of-all-trades."

The blacksmith had the same name as Karl's brother who would have finished his training and would also be a blacksmith by now. This coincidence awoke Karl's memories. As time passed, he did not think about his family as often as he once had, but at moments like this, he was reminded of them, and he felt the familiar nostalgic twinge associated with those memories. His family, his past was still a part of him, though it was far away and growing more dim with the passage of time.

After leaving the blacksmith shop, Isadore revealed that the blacksmith was the highest-paid man in the camp after Henry.

Heinrich wasn't surprised. "Wherever we go, we are the lowest paid. I think it's some kind of a law."

Isadore agreed. "Even the cooks. Course they work seven days a week. Oh, one last thing, that pine log." Isadore pointed to a long log laying in back of the bunk house, "That's the privy. Gets a little cold sometimes."

At supper time, the loggers that had made it to the camp assembled in the cook shanty. The cook shanty was really a combination of a cooking facility, dining hall, and storage for food items that should not freeze.

Henry announced the seating arrangements. "Those that picked seats before, go to them now."

After they had found their places, he directed, "New men today, pick a spot."

"All right, be seated."

When they were seated, Henry instructed them on dining hall etiquette.

"When you come into the dining hall, no one sits down until everyone is here. Everyone sits in the place they are at now. Nobody gets up to leave until everyone is done. No unnecessary talk. Start passing the food."

The cook shack was dimly lit by half a dozen kerosene lamps hung about the room. This room was large, thirty by forty feet, and this is where Steven and his two helpers satisfied the appetites of fifty-five men who required a lot of fuel to do strenuous physical work twelve hours a day in extremely cold weather. It was a large but cozy place, warmed by the large cooking range against the end wall and a large stove near the middle of the room. The room was always filled with the aroma of cooking food: bread baking, bacon frying, coffee perking. The walls of the dining hall were lined with open shelves filled with metal and enameled serving and eating plates, cups, utensils, coffee pots, and clay crocks, filled and unfilled. Food that couldn't be stored in the freezing dingle; potatoes, cabbages, fresh apples, were stored in sacks or bins on the floor under the shelves.

A two-level double bunk bed near the inner wall of the dining hall is where Steven and the two assistant cooks slept. They slept separately from the rest of the men because they kept different hours, having to get up much earlier than the rest of the camp to make breakfast.

# CHAPTER 17

▼

# LOGGING CAMP AT WORK

The following week, the lumberjacks started cutting trees in earnest. They worked from the time they could see the ends of their axes in the morning until they couldn't see them in the evening, six days a week.

The day started with the full crew going into the cook shanty for breakfast in the morning and leaving it as a group when they finished eating. After breakfast the teamsters would get the animals ready for the days work, and the lumberjacks marched to the work site carrying their saws and axes on their shoulders.

A foreman who oversaw the tree cutters led the march. His name was Kane. He was a New Englander who must have had poetical aspirations because he would make up ditties, calling out lines that the lumberjacks would repeat as they marched.

*It may be colder than a witch's tit*
*But it doesn't bother us a bit*
*We are rough,*
*We are tough*
*We cut wood for Flambeau number three*

*We have no fear of snow or ice*
*Just feed us lots of beans and rice*
*We are rough,*

*We are tough*
*We cut wood for Flambeau number three.*

The men would put a strong emphasis on the words rough and tough.

The lumberjacks worked in pairs, and naturally, Karl and Heinrich teamed up. They would notch the tree with an axe, then each would get on the end of a two-man saw and work together to saw through the trunk. Once the tree was felled, they would trim the log using their axes and then cut the trunk into lengths of sixteen to twenty feet, again using the two-man saw. The logs were gathered together by the men with the horses and oxen and dragged to a location where the logs would be loaded onto large sleds. The sleds were used to transport the logs to the river. A simple operation, repeated over and over throughout the northern winter.

It took Karl and Heinrich a couple of weeks to get used to the work and keep up with the veterans. Kane, the foreman, never said anything. It was obvious that many of the newer hands were straining, but apparently that was expected and tolerated as long as they giving it their best effort. It wasn't too long before Karl, Heinrich and the other new men were able to swing their axes with the best of them. It was much like the meat packing business. Once you got yourself into condition and learned the job, it did not seem that hard. The big difference was that Karl liked working out of doors in the fresh air, whereas he never learned to like the meat-packing work.

The lumberjacks represented a mixture of backgrounds and ethnic groups. A few were from back east—New England and Pennsylvania—and six were half-breed, French and Indian. The rest of the lumberjacks were recent immigrants, Scandinavians and Germans mostly. The teamsters, who brought their own horses or oxen to the camp, were farmers who lived in southern Wisconsin and Minnesota. They worked their farms in the summer and would spend the winter in the logging camp. Everyone except the French Indians were from somewhere else. The French Indians were descendants of the early French trappers and traders and native American women, a tough combination that adapted well to the lumberjack trade.

For many lumberjacks, working in the woods was something they did on the way to doing something else. Like Karl, they were working towards some goal beyond being lumberjacks.

Many camps had unique traditions and Flambeau No. Three had one that had been established when the camp opened three years before. No one seemed to know how it got started but it was known and observed by all the camp's lumberjacks. The tradition was that the French Indians would drop the first tree each morning when work started.

One cold morning, Heinrich was feeling extra good as they marched to the area they would be cutting that day. He had finished off a half dozen plate-sized pancakes covered with honey and current jam, a huge helping of bacon, an equally large helping of smoked ham, and a bowl of cooked prunes, all washed down with strong coffee. He was primed for a full morning of tree cutting.

"Karl, let's drop the first tree today," he suggested as they marched to the cutting area.

"We can't do that. The French Indians always drop the first tree."

"I think we should surprise them today."

"Why?"

"Hell, do you have to have a reason for everything? I just feel like doing it. We will walk right up to one of first trees to be cut, both work on the notch, like we were all warmed up, grab the sharp saw and saw through that trunk at sixty strokes a minute. We will drop it right on the lap of those French Indians before they wake up."

"That could cause trouble. They expect to drop the first tree."

"We can use a little excitement."

Karl was persuaded.

When they approached the cutting area, Karl and Heinrich shed their outer clothes and pulled off their gloves despite the minus ten degrees temperature. They stopped at one of the first trees to be cut that day, and started swinging their axes to notch the tree. Then grabbed the two-man saw and started pulling at it like their lives depended on it. In a few minutes they yelled, "Timber!" as the first tree of the day dropped.

The French Indians, just getting started on their first trees, were startled. They had been secure in the belief that no one would challenge them in dropping the day's first tree. They were so surprised that trees cut by other loggers started dropping around them before they got their first tree down.

Nothing was said by anyone.

When the tote arrived with the noon meal, Heinrich approached one of the French Indians.

The man looked Heinrich over suspiciously.

"Jean, sorry we almost dropped that tree on you this morning. We were just sawing away, not paying any attention to what we were doing, and it just dropped."

"You joke, no, a funny joke."

"No joke. Just not paying attention. Don't worry, after this we will have a smoke on our pipe and be sure the first tree drops before we saw anything down. Don't hurry."

The French Indians looked relieved once they were aware that their first-tree monopoly was not threatened, at least by Heinrich and Karl.

✳   ✳   ✳   ✳

Saturday nights and Sundays the men were able to rest and relax. They would play cards—Pinochle, poker, whist. There was a group that played checkers. Heinrich never had a desire to return to the Back of the Yards neighborhood, but some Saturday evenings he missed the dances at Packers Hall.

Isadore wasn't so sure it was the dances. "It's the women you are missing."

"Ya, maybe. Pinochle has its limits."

On some Saturday nights, a German with a squeeze box played folk tunes. A farmer from Pennsylvania had a fiddle and would play what he called mountain music.

One Saturday night a teamster who knew how to call a square dance asked the musicians if they knew any square dance tunes.

The fiddle player allowed that he knew a few, but the accordion player had never heard of such a thing.

"*Was ist dat*, sqvare dance?"

"I'll play, you follow," the fiddler instructed, and he played a tune.

The accordion player worked on it. He played by ear, and he was able to follow along after a couple of runs at a tune.

The teamster was ready to go. "All right, let's get some squares going here. First volunteers get to be men."

Five men who knew how to do squares stepped up.

"That will make one square unless we get three more women. We'll take learners."

Finally, Isadore stepped up. "Come on Karl, Heinrich. If you can't have one, you can be one."

Heinrich was game, Karl reluctant, but both ended up joining the group as learners.

They tied on flower-sack aprons to identify themselves as women.

There was a lot of confusion, but things got better with practice, and Karl and Heinrich were introduced to the American square dance. More joined in after it got started, and they kept going for a couple of hours.

Heinrich had to admit it was fun, even if he had to be a woman.

Talking was another diversion. Conversations could cover a wide range of subjects, due in part to the diverse backgrounds of the lumberjacks.

If one was interested in an intellectual discussion, there was a bookish fellow named Albert. He had carried in as many books as he was able and shared the limited library Henry had in his room. He was fluent in English, German, and French. Karl could never understand what he was doing in a lumber camp.

Albert also kept a journal, and he wrote in it every day. Heinrich asked him why.

"Keep track of what happened everyday."

"I don't need a journal to do that. I cut down trees yesterday, the day before, and the day before that."

"Maybe someday I will write a book about logging camps."

"Who would want to read about logging camps?" Karl asked, then added, "Who would believe it?"

"It would be fiction, make-believe."

"That might work."

There was another German, a fellow named Armond, with kinky blond hair. He was in his middle twenties, talked a lot and had strong viewpoints on a lot of subjects. He was the antithesis of an intellectual, however. He was sure he knew everything about everything and took positions he considered unassailable on just about any subject you could think of.

One evening, Heinrich and Isadore were talking about thunderstorms, particularly Chicago thunderstorms and how violent they often were. Albert had overheard the conversation and asked, "Do you know what makes it thunder?"

Armond, who was within hearing distance, had the answer. "God makes thunder. Everybody knows that."

"Not directly. Lightning heating up the air makes it thunder."

"That's a lie. God makes thunder. That's the only way thunder is made."

Albert went back to the book he had been reading, choosing to ignore the challenge to his statement. Armond was not going to be ignored. He grabbed Albert by the shoulders and shouted, "Only God makes thunder. Admit it."

Albert gave him a perplexed look. "What's wrong with you?"

Whereupon Armond grabbed Albert by the neck and started choking him. Two lumberjacks grabbed Armond by the arms, carried him out the door and threw him into a snowbank. That was the way minor flare-ups were often handled, and it usually worked to cool things down.

Isadore advised the bookish German, "You got something different to put in your journal today."

Armond had noticed Karl joking with Steven, the Negro cook. He questioned Karl."You a nigger-lover, Karl?"

"Women. Women are what I like."

"I saw you joking with that nigger cook."

"We get along."

"I bet you get along with Jews too. Goddamn Christ killers and niggers, they are even up here in the woods."

Armond wasn't alone in his views. One of the cook's helpers shared Armond's dislike for Negroes, but he held that bias pretty close for obvious reasons. He was named Jon and had grown up in Pennsylvania. His parents had moved from Virginia when he was a little child. They had been southern sympathizers, and he had apparently retained much of that which they had taught him. He was a big man, but not as big as Steven. Armond and Jon had conversations about the "nigger problem."

Friction among the lumber camp workers was rare. They put so much energy into the work to be done that there was little left over for anything else. Another factor was the absence of alcohol. After the first few weeks there was little if any alcohol in the camp. However, with a volatile mix of young men living in close quarters, there is always the potential for conflict.

On some Saturday nights, after the cooks finished cleaning up, Steven would come over and join one of the card games if there was an opening. On one particular Saturday night, there was an opening at a table where Armond was playing. Steven filled the empty stump at the table, whereupon Armond jumped up and angrily proclaimed that he didn't want any "Goddamn nigger" playing at his table, and for Steven to "get the hell out of there." Steven continued to sit and calmly asked the dealer for some cards.

Armond was beside himself. "Nigger, didn't you hear me? Get the hell away from this table."

Steven ignored him. By this time all the eyes in the bunk house were on the confrontation. Nobody intervened; the snow-bank treatment did not seem to fit the situation. Armond walked over to Steven and grabbed him by the shoulders to pull him away from the table. It was like grabbing onto a large boulder. There was no give. Frustrated, Armond doubled up his fist and struck Steven on the ear.

Jon, who had been observing the activity, got carried away, and forgetting his delicate job situation, grabbed Steven from behind. "Nigger, you heard. Move away from the table."

Steven could not ignore the antagonists any longer. Rising up, he threw Jon down on his back and at the same time swung the back of his hand into Armond's face and sent him sprawling. Jon raised himself to a sitting position. His blood was really up now. He reached into his boot, pulled out a knife, jumped up, and charged Steven. Steven ignored the knife, threw out his arm full length, and sunk his fist into Jon's midriff. Jon dropped, gasping for air.

A couple of men that held views similar to Armond's jumped in and piled onto Steven, who brushed them away like annoying insects. Men who had been on the fence now joined in the effort to subdue Steven. No one sided with Steven.

A shot rang out.

Henry was standing in the doorway of the bunkhouse, a pistol in his hand. All activity ceased and the men turned to face him.

"All right, let's settle down. There will be none of this going on in this camp. It's time for everyone to turn in for the night. Steven, go to the cook shanty. We will sort this out in the morning."

There was no dissent. The situation called for someone to be in charge, and in this camp, that was Henry. The camp foreman was much like a captain of a ship at sea. Isolated by a distance of days from outside assistance, Henry had to maintain order if it was threatened.

The men turned in. All went to their usual places except Jon, who for obvious reasons decided not to bunk in the cook shanty.

The next day was Sunday, a non-work day, and a good time for Henry to handle the bunk room disturbance.

First he called in Karl and got his version of the event. Next he talked to Heinrich and one other non-participant. He talked to Steven, Armond, and Jon

Later that day, right after the noon meal, Armond and Jon were outfitted with snowshoes for overland winter travel. They packed enough supplies to get themselves back to Eau Claire. Finally, Henry gave each of them a slip of paper which indicated the number of days they had worked. Upon turning that into the office at Eau Claire, they would be paid for the work they had done. They had been given the choice of snowshoes or waiting for the tote that would be making a journey to Eau Claire for supplies next week. They chose the snowshoes.

Most of the men, regardless of their biases, had to agree that justice had been done.

During the next few days, Isadore, Karl, and Heinrich discreetly made the camp aware of Steven's distaste for the word "nigger," and the word was used cautiously in that camp for the rest of the winter. Everyone agreed on one thing. That "nigger" was one hell of a man.

The camp returned to normal. On some Saturday nights, Steven would show up in the bunkhouse and join in a card game. He was always welcomed.

The Steven incident dwelled in Karl's mind. Karl had found racial friction to be common in America. There seemed to be friction between every ethnic group: Irish, Poles, Italians, Germans, and most of all, Negroes. Karl talked to Heinrich about this phenomena. Heinrich didn't think it was any different in America than in Prussia, or anywhere else. "In Prussia you have Poles and Jews, both outcasts as far as Prussians are concerned. The only difference in America is that you have everything here. There are more things to have friction about."

"Ya, that's true," Karl agreed. "But since there are so many different people here, you would think the differences wouldn't be so important?"

"I don't think it works that way. People get put in boxes. Like all Negroes are inferior people to be avoided, all Indians are savages to be hunted down. People who look different or talk different don't mix well. It's in people's nature to be that way."

For the most part, from what Karl had observed, what Heinrich was saying was true. However, there were questions in Karl's mind about Heinrich's assumption that it had to be that way. Are people who look different and talk different really all that differen? Karl was sure that all people felt pain or joy in the same way and that all their blood was the same color. They all laugh or smile when they heard a funny story or joke. Down below the surface, Karl was sure people were all pretty much the same. Karl reminded Heinrich of the women they met on the beach in Chicago. "I said they lived in a different world, and you said, 'Ya, but they are still people, those women are no different than peasant girls when you get right down to it.' I think you were right, and I think that differences between different groups is the same thing. When you get right down to it, we are all just people. We may look different and talk different, but in other ways we are all the same."

"Ya," Heinrich laughed. "We are all bigots."

Karl was still struggling with his thoughts. "I'm not sure that is true Heinrich, maybe we are just ignorant. Take Steven, once you get to know him, he is just like a regular guy. I like him, consider him a friend. There are some Negroes I probably wouldn't like, not because they were Negroes but because like some Germans I know, I wouldn't like them for other reasons."

Heinrich was ready to change the subject. "Karl, you are making my head hurt. Lets talk about something we know something about."

Karl agreed. They were getting beyond their depth.

*         *         *         *

The camp had fallen into a regular routine by the middle of December. They were working in an excellent stand of pine trees, and all the men were in shape and putting their full effort into the task.

Karl was noticing a camaraderie developing in the camp similar to what he had experienced in the army. They were a group of men living together in close quarters who ate the same food, shared the same experiences, and were working together to achieve a common end. A bond and trust was developing and each knew he could depend on the other.

Despite their satisfaction with the lumber camp, Karl and Heinrich knew this work was only a bridge to take them to something more permanent. Karl's long-time goal remained unchanged. Heinrich's goal was less certain, but he also knew he would be moving on, probably to follow Karl and see what would develop. That had been his pattern so far and it had been an interesting, if not a lucrative experience.

In late January the haulers were falling behind, so Karl, Heinrich, and some of the other cutters were told to help work off the surplus of fallen logs. They cleared paths through the woods so the teamsters could snake fallen logs out to be loaded. They helped load the sleds that were carrying the logs to the river.

Logs are heavy, and there was no way to lift them onto to the sleds. Rolling them was the only option. A ramp was made using two timbers where one end of each timber was on the ground and the other end on the sled. Then a pair of log chains was placed around the log to be loaded. One end of each chain was attached to a tree standing on the opposite side of the sled from the ramp. The other ends were attached to the yoke of a pair of oxen. When the oxen moved forward, the chains would tighten around the log, and it would start rolling up the timber ramp and onto the sled. They would start out with small logs to stabilize the sled. Once that was accomplished, they could load anything the oxen could move. The sleds, pulled by two teams hitched in tandem, could haul tremendous loads of logs on iced tracks that were maintained by a sprinkler sleigh.

A couple of weeks into this new line of work, Karl was helping load a sled. The teamster on each sled hauling logs would determine how large a load should be, and some teamsters relished hauling the biggest load. The teamster with the sled Karl was loading was one of these. They had loaded the sled with what would have been a normal load and were expecting the teamster to say "enough," but he didn't. The tote bringing the noon meal arrived. Finally, after loading one more log and attaining what had to be the largest load for the day, the teamster finally said, "Enough."

Karl took hold of a log chain that had been pulled over the load and ran one end through a holding ring on the sleigh. He secured the chain's hook in a link and was going to tighten the chain when the load suddenly gave way. The chain snapped like a piece of string and the logs began to cascade off the sled. Karl attempted to jump clear but one arm became pinched between two logs. Something snapped, his arm came free, and he was able to get clear before the whole load crashed down on him.

Karl had fallen backward when he pulled free and ended up on his back in the snow with a sharp pain piercing his left arm. He looked at the arm and could see, even with the arm encased in his jacket, that it was at an impossible angle. It took a moment for Karl to realize what must have happened. What now? Karl recalled that in the army there had been medics and doctors in the field to take care of things like this. In the Wisconsin woods there was nothing like that.

The full crew had gathered for the noon meal when the accident occurred. Henry came running over, arriving soon after the logs had finished tumbling off the sled. He saw Karl lying in the snow.

"You all right Karl?" He called.

"Not quite. Something wrong with my arm."

Henry looked at it, muttered, "Oh oh," and shouted, "Get the tote over here!"

After getting back to the camp, Henry pulled off Karl's jacket, cut his shirt sleeve open, and then confirmed the obvious: a broken arm, the large bone in the forearm. It was not a compound fracture, but by feeling the arm Henry could tell that the bone was fully broken. In his many years of experience in lumber camps, Henry had seen many accidents, and as foreman had to deal with them. Although the arm was turning black and blue and was pretty ugly, it was a fracture that should not be difficult to set.

"Well, Karl, here is what we can do: try to set it here, or have a tote take you back to Eau Claire. The tote would take four days if the weather is good. I have set bones before. This one looks pretty straightforward."

The choices were not good ones. Either wait several days before tending to the break, or have a novice set it. Karl took a big breath and put his trust in Henry.

"Go ahead, set it."

Henry had splints made and had the cooks work up a batch of plaster to be used for a cast. He dug up some gauze and a bottle of whiskey that had been stashed away in his office for this kind of an emergency. Steven was enlisted to help set the bone. Henry washed the arm throughly, then poured a generous portion of whiskey for Karl to drink. He gave Steven directions on how to apply his strength to move the bone back to its normal position. Karl braced himself when Henry told Steven to pull. The pain became overwhelming, and Karl felt himself descending into darkness and passed out. The splints were being applied before he had fully revived.

Henry finished up the splinting and applied the plaster for the cast. "I think we have it back pretty much as it was originally. Just needs time to heal."

When finished, the arm cast looked almost professional. Karl still felt pain, but the worst was over.

"How's it feel?" Henry asked after finishing up.

"Sore as hell."

"It will be sore for a while. Seemed to set pretty good. Time will tell. You will be in the cast for about six weeks, then a sling for a few more weeks. You will be ready to go about the time we break camp."

That was something that Karl had not thought about. What was he going to do for the next two months?

"What am I supposed to do Henry? I can't swing an axe with one arm. I don't know what I would do if I rode the tote back to Eau Claire."

"That's right, you are kind of stuck. Don't worry, you have a place to sleep, eat. We can't pay you, but you won't be out in the cold."

It suddenly occurred to Karl that his plans to homestead land next spring had just been delayed again.

*     *     *     *

Karl tried to make himself useful. He helped the cooks, manned the wanigan and carried in wood for the stoves with his one good arm. He took walks in the woods. One day he tried out some snowshoes, and soon he was traveling over the snow away from the packed trails where he had been confined before. His experience in the woods up to this time had been oriented around his work where he concentrated on the tree being cut down, not on the forest. Snow had been something to push through, useful to transport logs, made unsightly by the lumber men's activities. His snowshoe forays revealed a different world. Snow covered the landscape and clung to the pine branches, transforming the forest with a camouflage of purity. He saw the tall straight pines as things of beauty, not objects to be cut down.

One day he came upon a particularly tall stand of white pine with a canopy so tight that there was little undergrowth in the open space under them. The tall tree trunks reached straight for the sky. Karl recalled how Henry had said that places in the virgin forest reminded him of a cathedral, and now Karl could see the same image. He followed animal tracks and startled snowshoe rabbits, chased a grouse out of its snow house, and observed where deer had dug down to find tender browse on the forest floor. The forest was filled with activities that he had not been aware of.

Observing nature undisturbed by men and their enterprises was a new experience for Karl. He became aware that he was troubled by the realization that what he was looking at would soon be turned into slash and stumps. He knew his job depended on destroying what seemed so beautiful, and yet he felt the work he and others were doing was for a good purpose. You cannot have both, the beauty of a standing forest and lumbering, there is a choice be made. The choice had been made to cut down this forest, certainly not by him, but he was helping to implement that choice. It troubled him, but it was a dilemma he could not resolve.

\*     \*     \*     \*

One day, while Karl was tidying up the wanagin, the file man came over and started talking to him about learning to set and sharpen saws. This was a little surprising. Filers were paid a premium and did not readily share their knowledge with others.

Ben was the file man's name. He was a Pennsylvania farmer who had spent his winters in the logging camps for many years, but he was tiring of it and this would be his last year. Training in a replacement was a reasonable thing to do, and he wondered if Karl was interested in learning the skill.

Of course. Why not? Learning the saw-filer skill opened up the opportunity to earn premium pay, not to mention doing more comfortable and less strenuous work than manhandling trees all day.

Ben began tutoring Karl on the technique and art of saw sharpening. Karl quickly learned it was more complicated and challenging than he had imagined it to be.

Ben gave him a little introduction to what was expected of a file man. "The file man job is one of the most important in the camp, as important as the cook's."

"That important?" Karl questioned.

"That's right, if the saws aren't sharp, set right, it slows the whole camp down. Believe me, if the saws aren't sharpened right, the lumberjacks know it. The saws will grab, cut slow."

Ben went on to explain that there were four main procedures: jointing, shaping, setting, and filing. Filing sharpened the saw, and was done to every saw returned by the lumberjacks at the end of the work day. Jointing, shaping, and setting would be done depending on the condition of the saw. Jointing flattens or evens out the teeth along the length of the saw. If the jointing procedure has been done, the teeth have to be shaped. Shaping makes the teeth uniform. Setting provides a kerf that is wider than the thickness of the blade and ensures that the saw will not grab. Setting may not have to be done after a light sharpening, but it is always needed after jointing and shaping.

"It's a craft," Ben explained. "You can learn it, but a little natural ability helps. There's good filers and some that are not so good."

The left hand on the broken arm was free enough to aid the more crucial right hand in the sharpening process. Ben soon saw that Karl had the talent needed to be a good filer and he was soon sharpening and setting saws to Ben's standards.

After learning the technique, Karl did a good portion of the sharpening for the remainder of the season, and Ben got to take things easy during his last few weeks of work.

By the middle of March they could no longer use the sleds to haul logs. The ice was turning to mud, and the logging of trees was shut down. Most of the loggers headed out of the woods, but a crew remained to shut down the camp and get the logs into the river so the spring floods and river rats could drive them down to the mills.

Karl, Heinrich, and Isadore were among those chosen to stay on for the cleanup work. By the end of April their work was done. Before leaving camp they made arrangements to be back for the coming winter's logging and with Karl as the file man.

# CHAPTER 18

▼

# OUT OF THE WOODS

Each spring, thousands of hearty, virile lumberjacks with a winter's pay in their pockets were turned loose on the frontier logging towns. It made the logging towns some of the most exciting, dangerous, lustful, falling-down-drunk places in the world for several weeks each spring.

Many lumberjacks came out of the woods with a destination well in mind and in a hurry to get there. Ben the file man was one of them. He was anxious to get back to his Pennsylvania farm and caught the first available train out of town. Isadore had made arrangements with a teamster to work on his farm downstate during the summer. But others did not have firm plans, and the sudden availability of free time, alcohol, and women for the first time in months overwhelmed the coping skills of many lumberjacks.

Karl was well aware of these temptations when they returned to Eau Claire, and he was determined to remain calm and use good judgement. Heinrich was less inclined to fight the devil, but was influenced to some degree by his more principled friend.

The first order of business was to find a room to spend a few days until they figured out what they would be doing during the coming summer. Going back to Chicago was not high on the list of things they wanted to do. They would check out the local possibilities and go from there.

There were three hotels in Eau Claire. Karl and Heinrich not only found the daily rates seasonally inflated, but worse yet, the hotels all filled. Spring was the hotels peak season due to the influx of lumberjacks from the north woods and bolstered by some enterprising madams who would rent blocks of rooms to be used intermittently.

They checked the rooming houses next. They were at the opposite end of the spectrum, offering to only rent rooms for a month, minimum.

"Looks like we find ourselves a place under a tree and make do," Heinrich offered after they had spent a good part of the day in search of a place to park themselves and their gear.

He spotted a store that sold dry goods, women's and men's clothing. "Let's stop in there. These clothes aren't going to make it much further."

They found a woman named Patty in sole charge of the store that afternoon. She had red hair, was forty-something in age, and appeared well maintained.

Karl and Heinrich had not shaved, bathed, or washed their clothes since last fall. Whenever they moved anywhere near Patty, they could see her backing up.

"Just get out of the woods?" Patty asked, needlessly, because the evidence to support that was plain to the senses.

"Yes ma'am," Heinrich volunteered.

"Looks like you need pretty much everything."

"Guess we look a little shabby."

New flannel shirts, blue jeans, and underwear were picked out.

After selecting the clothing items, Karl decided that asking about a place to room might be worthwhile.

"Ma'am, do you know where we might find a room for a few days?"

"I really don't know of any rooms. They are pretty well filled up this time of the year."

"We found out."

Patty totaled up their purchases and found a sack to put the clothes in.

She seemed a little distracted, then offered, "I have an extra room. I could help you out for a few days."

Karl did not hesitate, "We will take it. How much?"

Patty had not thought about that. "I really don't know. I've never rented it out."

Karl asked, "How about eighty cents a day?" He knew that was more than the normal room rate, but things were not normal right now.

"We will pay you for five days up-front. We should need it about two weeks."

"That sounds fair. Would you want to see it first?"

"We were thinking of sleeping under a tree. I'm sure it will do."

"Your names are?"

"Karl Mueller, and this is Heinrich Schlicter."

"I'm Patty, Patty O'Neal."

They agreed to meet at the store when she closed at five, and she would show them the way to her home.

After leaving, Heinrich gave Karl a friendly poke. "Who would have thought we would find a room in a dry goods store? I wonder if she has a tub. Soaking off the crud might be a good idea."

"Now that you mention it, let's find a laundry and get this pack of dirty clothes cleaned up."

They found a laundry and emptied their bags of a big part of their contents. Their clothes would be ready in a day.

"So," Karl was wondering, "what shall we do for the next couple of hours, look at job prospects for the summer?"

"I'm thinking having a few beers would make more sense. When is the last time you had a beer?"

"I had a shot of whiskey when I had my arm set."

"That don't count."

"Maybe a beer would be a good idea."

They didn't have to go far to find a saloon. Every other place on the street seemed to be one.

The interior was fairly narrow, but deep, with a long bar and a row of tables occupying the front half and more tables devoted to gambling in the back. There was the universal odor of stale beer and cigar smoke. It was mid-afternoon, and because unemployed lumberjacks weren't tied to any fixed schedule, there was a pretty good crowd in the saloon.

As luck would have it, there were two lumberjacks sitting at a table that had spent the winter at Flambeau No. Three. They ordered a pitcher and joined them. There was a lot of nothing to talk about and another pitcher was ordered. Karl got up to go to the privy and discovered he was actually a little tipsy. He had not eaten lunch, and his long abstinence from alcohol had apparently lowered his tolerance substantially. But they had to have one more pitcher, that was for sure. Time seemed to be standing still until Heinrich suddenly exclaimed, "What the hell, it's past five. We lost our room."

They grabbed their bags, and though a little foggy in the head, made an impressive dash up the street, considering that they were wearing heavy boots and had large packs bouncing on their backs.

It was almost five thirty. There was a closed sign hanging in the door. "Closed" was an English word both of them could read.

"Oh shit," Karl gasped as they stood panting by the door.

The door opened a crack and Patty O'Neal peered out at them. "You are lucky I had some straightening up to do."

Karl apologized, "Sorry. The time sort of got away from us."

Patty wasn't acting real angry. "You looked pretty funny, running up the street with all that gear flopping around."

Her home was not far away, and the room was better than they were expecting. It was upstairs, a good-sized room with a double bed. Everything was clean. The facilities were out back. She had a large bathtub downstairs that she said they could use, telling them that they had to heat the water on the stove, and dump the water out back when they finished.

They moved right in, and the big clean up was next on the list of things to do. Heinrich went first. Patty helped heat water for the tub and asked him if he wanted to have his clothes washed.

"Think they can be saved?"

"If the dirt isn't holding them together."

"You're welcome to try it."

When Heinrich finished bathing, he put on the new clothes. He felt so good, and so clean that he was almost beside himself. He had to get back on the street and check out the town. He told Karl he would meet him in the saloon at the end of the street.

"No more saloons for me. I'll meet you in that eating place right next door."

Heinrich agreed.

Patty helped heat the water for Karl's bath and repeated the instructions to leave his dirty clothes if he wanted them washed.

"How long were you up in the woods?" Patty asked.

"Since late last November."

"That's a long time."

"Sure is."

Patty left and Karl peeled off his dirty clothes, got into the tub, and let the feeling of water soaking into his pores fill his body. He must have lain almost motionless for twenty minutes before he decided to soap up. The water was growing a little tepid. He thought, "Dare I ask?" then called, "Patty, could I have another pail of hot water? Just set it inside the door."

She called back, "It will be a few minutes."

In a few minutes, the door opened, and she came in carrying the bucket. "I'll just pour it in," she said and walked over and let it slowly drain into the tub.

Patty had changed into something different, a loosely fitting gown.

Karl could see a partially exposed breast through the loose front opening of the gown as she poured in the water.

Patty finished pouring, then asked, "Would you like to have me wash your back?"

Karl was now fully awake and saw unexpected possibilities taking shape. Patty was an older woman, maybe not the woman of his dreams, but obviously female.

"That would be nice," he managed.

She helped him dry. He wrapped the towel about his middle and followed her into her bedroom. It didn't take long to release his pent-up virility and he lay happily exhausted. Suddenly, he remembered that he was supposed to meet Heinrich.

He started to get up, but Patty held him, "Don't leave."

"I have to. Heinrich is waiting."

"Heinrich can take care of himself."

"I said I would meet him."

"When you come back, sleep here."

"You sure?"

"Yes."

The street was busy now, with groups and individuals exploring the offerings or moving from one bar to another.

There was no Heinrich at the eating place, but Karl was starved and ordered up a lumberjack-sized supper. When he was finished, there was still no Heinrich. Patty was right, Heinrich could take care of himself. He lingered over a cup of coffee and lit up his pipe.

Karl was about to leave when Heinrich came in with a plain, good sized-blonde woman.

"Karl, I waited a while. Thought you had forgotten me. This is Heidi. Heidi, this is Karl. Did you eat? How about you Heidi, want something to eat?"

Heidi would have something to eat. Karl had eaten, but would have another cup of coffee. Heinrich ordered some food for himself.

Heidi was from Minnesota and had ridden the stage over from Saint Paul a couple of months ago with two other girls. They wanted to check out Eau Claire, where they heard there was plenty of action this time of the year. Heidi had grown up on a Minnesota farm, but had been on her own in the big city of Saint Paul for about a year. Heidi worked in the corner bar, and yes, there had been plenty of action since she got here.

Heidi left to go to the privy and Heinrich filled Karl in further.

"Man, that woman can turn you inside out. I just made up for six months in the woods in an hour. You should try that."

Karl smiled mysteriously. "You know that kind of stuff doesn't bother me. I can take it or leave it."

Heinrich studied Karl. "You lie."

Heidi had returned and sat down beside Karl. She moved close to him and laid her hand on his leg.

"Karl, what is it you missed most up in the woods?" she asked. She moved her hand back and forth.

Karl thought about that for a while, then allowed that what he probably missed most of all was having a beer or two Saturdays evenings with friends. "I used to think about that when I was in the woods, all the time."

Heidi gave Karl an odd look. She didn't know how to proceed. She removed her hand from Karl's leg and mentioned something about needing to get back to the bar next door.

Heinrich peered at his friend and had to admit a new level of respect. "You really can take it or leave it. You weren't kidding, were you?"

While walking back to their accommodations, Karl filled Heinrich in.

Heinrich exclaimed, "You big fake! What a hell of a deal. We are friends, share and share alike."

"It's not mine to share."

"You can put in a good word."

"Somewhere we draw the line, and it is somewhere before that."

Karl did not fully understand Patty, or their relationship, but he liked what he knew about it so far. He eventually found out that Patty was a widow. Her husband had been killed in a mill accident. She had one daughter who lived in Illinois. She didn't have any reason to stay in Eau Claire, but no reason to leave either. She had the house, a job, enough to get by.

She was curious, asking what Karl thought of his seducer.

"You are a very attractive woman."

"Beyond that."

"You surprised me."

"I surprised myself. I have never done anything like that before. When you and Heinrich came in that day, I can't imagine what could have attracted me. The odor was pretty bad. Maybe I was just curious to know what was under all that crud and dirt, wanted to see it cleaned up."

Their search for summer work was aided by chance and Henry, their well-connected friend. They ran into Henry on the street in Eau Claire, and he informed them that the logging company he worked for was going to build a new camp further up the Flambeau. Logging camps were continually being built to replace those abandoned in areas where the forest had been depleted.

Henry instructed them, "A crew is being put together right now. Go down to the company office, give them my name, and they will put you on."

They followed Henry's directions, and as he predicted, were hired on for the summer's work.

In less than two weeks they were ready to go back in the woods for the summer to help build the logging camp.

The time in Eau Claire had been short, but during that time Karl's sensual knowledge had expanded greatly.

Heinrich noted the apparent strain. "You have been lounging around and eating like a horse, and looking more peaked every day."

Karl answered him with a smile, a satisfied smile.

# CHAPTER 19

▼

# BACK TO WORK

Construction of the new logging camp consisted of cutting trees and using the logs to form the walls of buildings for a new camp. Finished lumber for the roof and floors was brought in over a trail they helped hack through the forest.

The camp was being built in the middle of a standing virgin forest, and the scent of pine trees filled the air. A good-sized lake teeming with fish was just down the hill from the camp. A cow moose and her calf could be seen browsing in the shallows of the lake most mornings. Surrounding the new lumber camp was a forest of white pine trees with straight trunks rising a hundred feet into the air supporting a canopy of needled branches. The ground under the closely packed pines was bare except for a soft mattress of fallen pine needles. Where blow-downs caused breaks in the canopy, the forest was being renewed by young saplings growing among a profusion of wild flowers.

Once again, as in the past winter when he had time to wander the forest, Karl was struck by the beauty of the standing forest.

He talked to Heinrich about his thoughts.

"Ya," Heinrich agreed. "It's pretty alright, but what's it good for? These trees are only worth something when you make lumber out of them."

Karl wasn't so sure. "Seems like a forest like this is worth something, just standing like it is."

"For what? Heinrich replied. "Who is going to pay you to look at a forest? They will pay you to cut it down, that's for sure."

They earned a dollar a day for a twelve-hour day, six days a week, plus room and board, and they thought it was the best job they had ever had.

It was soon fall and they returned to Eau Claire to get ready for the coming winter at Flambeau No. Three. Karl paid a visit to the dry goods store where Patty O'Neal worked. She was still there and blushed deeply when she saw Karl.

"Is the room for rent?" Karl asked, hopefully.

Patty averted her eyes. "I'm planning to be married next month. Another Carl. He spells it with a 'C'. He works at the Northwest mill."

Karl was obviously disappointed, but not totally surprised. Women were revered and scarce in this part of the world. "I'm happy for you. That Carl, he is a lucky man." Karl was sincere and meant every word of it.

Patty smiled. "Thank you. I will never forget you."

Heinrich was disappointed also. It would be hard to duplicate those accommodations.

They found a room in a hotel. The hotels were now on a normal schedule, and rooms were reasonable compared to the spring craziness.

They were now veterans and knew what to expect as they prepared themselves for the annual trek to the winter camp.

Heinrich had become acquainted with an Irishman, Pat McGinnis, another patron of the corner saloon. They enjoyed each other's company and occasionally got together to discuss the world's problems. One day they were talking about the pros and cons of different jobs. Pat worked in the Northwest Company Sawmill, making a dollar and a half a day. He worked twelve hours a day during the week, ten hours on Saturdays and had Sundays off.

Pat preferred working in the mills. "I don't know if I could go all winter without my ale. I need that almost everyday to keep the throat from drying out. Women, that would be a problem, too. Germans and Swedes probably don't have those kinds of problems."

Heinrich had to admit that the social life in the camps was limited. It was definitely a drawback. "Everybody has those kinds of problems from what I can tell, some more than others. Ya, it is a problem for everyone."

"Why don't you work in the mill?" Pat asked. "You have to pay your own board and room, but they pay you more too. You end up about the same after you figure everything out. If the pay is the same, why go up in the woods all winter? That's what I figure."

"Guess I never thought about it much," Heinrich answered. "Could I get work in the mill?"

"Hey, you bet you can get a job. Old Pat has pull at the mill."

Heinrich mentioned the possibility to Karl. "Did you ever think about working in the mills? Pat says you can end up with about the same amount of money working in the mill, and he can get us in."

Karl ran the idea through his mind, but he had the file man's job this coming winter. He made as much as the mill paid plus room and board so it did not seem attractive financially. Besides, he really did like being in the woods. It had its drawbacks, that is for sure, but for him it was the best choice. "You do what you have to do, Heinrich, but camp is where I will be this winter. I have the file man's job, that is one thing, and I guess I prefer the camp to Eau Claire, strange as that might sound."

Heinrich laughed. "Since I don't have the file man's job and I am of sound mind, I guess I will see if Pat can really get me a job in the mill."

It turned out that Pat did not have the pull needed to get Heinrich a job, but there was work in another mill that paid the same. Heinrich decided to take the job and stay in Eau Claire.

After Karl departed for camp he soon missed Heinrich's wit and presence. It seemed that some part of his own being was missing. It occurred to him that he and Heinrich had been constant companions for over four years and had shared many experiences, even the same bed, during that time. They had never had a real dispute. Minor disagreements sometimes, which were usually ended when Heinrich made some funny, or self-deprecating remark about the matter. Heinrich would be missed. Maybe next spring Heinrich would join him when he set out to find land to homestead. He hoped so.

Karl found the saw filer's job demanding, but not in the same way as working as a lumberjack in the woods. There was more skill and less physical activity involved in the work, which fit Karl's disposition, and the extra pay was a bonus.

In reviewing his finances once more, he now expected to have around $350 next spring, counting what he would earn that winter and what he had in the Chicago savings account.

Karl knew most of the teamsters. They tended to stick together as might be expected. They were doing the same kind of work and most came from similar circumstances. They were farmers first and loggers second, so they talked a lot about farming when they got together. Karl found the talk interesting and informative. He listened mostly and asked questions occasionally. He felt like he had a lot to learn.

One day the conversation turned to homesteading. One of the teamsters was thinking of pulling up stakes and homesteading some land in western Minnesota or in the Dakota territory. He was tired of clearing stumps from the land he was farming and thought he might do better starting fresh.

Curious, Karl asked him what he felt he needed to homestead land. What kind of investment would he need to make.

"I have a wagon, tools, animals, enough for sure. Don't plan to need anything more, for now."

"What if you started from scratch? How much money would you need?" Karl asked.

A couple of other teamsters weighed in. One had an opinion. "If you are starting from scratch and you need horses, tools, and breed stock, I would guess six to eight hundred dollars, something like that, minimum."

Karl was shocked. "You sure?"

Other teamsters shook their heads affirmatively, and substantiated the first teamster's estimate.

One added, "If you have a claim, and some money to put down on things you need to buy, like animals, tools, there are lenders that will loan you money, using what you buy or the preemption as collateral."

"Preemption?"

"After a claim is made, the land can be proved up after six months for a dollar twenty five cents an acre. Some lenders will gamble that the land will be worth more than that."

Another teamster added, "Homesteading and borrowing money is a gamble, but what the hell isn't? You are gambling that you are going to make a crop and generate some cash the first year."

Karl realized he had to reassess his assumptions. His long-held estimate of the money needed to homestead land was badly out of whack. He was hearing he would need to have twice as much money as he would likely have that following spring. Making what he was now, it would take him another two years if that new amount was the right one. Always two more years. He would run out of years before he ever homesteaded some land. He decided he would set out after he finished up at the logging camp this coming spring. He would go with whatever he had and use credit if he needed it. He couldn't delay his plans any longer.

# C H A P T E R   20

▼

# A DETOUR

By mid-March the cutting and hauling was shut down. Karl once more stayed on to close down the camp and get the logs into the river.

At the end of April, Karl found Heinrich still working in the mill in Eau Claire where he had left him the previous fall. As expected, Heinrich invited Karl to move in with him, solving his temporary housing problem.

Karl had hardly moved in when Heinrich started talking about a wild idea he and Pat had. They were going to head out west to the Black Hills in the Dakota territory. Gold had been discovered, and they were going out there to get some of it.

"Karl, they are panning a hundred dollars a day out of the creeks! It is just getting started. There's gold that's has been found, and there is more to be found. If we get out there this summer, we will be in on the beginning of it."

It took Karl a while to digest what he was hearing. "Where did you hear about this?"

"Pat reads the newspaper. He read about it in the Chicago paper, other people have been talking about it. A General Custer found gold there a couple of years ago. Then this past summer prospectors found lots of it in a different part of the hills. That is what Pat says."

"Sounds kind of crazy to me." Karl pronounced. "What do you know about gold mining? What does Pat know about gold?"

"We know it is worth a lot. Other than that, not much, but you don't need to know much. What you need to do is stake a claim with gold in it, then you can figure out how to sort it out. Getting the gold out of the ground is not that hard. Finding ground with gold in it and laying claim to that ground is the important part."

"All right," conceded Karl. "So what makes you think you can find a claim with gold in it?"

"We figure we have as good a chance as the next man," Heinrich answered. "What about joining us? You were going to go west to homestead. This is west, west of here somewhere."

The idea was just too new and too strange for Karl to give any kind of answer. Karl's response was not enthusiastic. "Sounds a little far-fetched for me. Can't say I'd be interested. I don't even know where those hills are, never heard of them before."

Heinrich persisted, "Tell you what. Pat and I usually get together at the corner saloon Saturday night. Why don't you join us tomorrow night for a beer anyway?"

"Sure, why not?" Karl agreed.

The following evening, Karl, Heinrich, and Pat met at the corner saloon to have a beer and talk about the future. None of them had ever intended lumbering to be their life's work. It was jsut a job to take them to the next step. The next step for Karl, although long delayed, was well defined. Heinrich and Pat did not have a wel-formed goal. Their plans were something like wait until a good opportunity came along and then go for it. The Black Hills gold rush seemed to fit the bill.

Pat had gotten most of his information about the gold rush from the Chicago news paper, and he had found more information in a geography book they had at the small Eau Claire library. Pat filled Heinrich and Karl in on what he had learned. "Those hills and the whole Dakota territory had been by passed by settlers heading west on the Oregon Trail. Same thing when the Pacific Union Railroad was built. The government figured since nobody seemed to want that part of the country, why not give it to the Indians? So everything in the Dakota territory west of the Missouri River, including the Black Hills, is now Indian territory. The Custer expedition found some gold in the Black Hills in '74, then prospectors found more in '75. Now there is a bunch of interest in the Black Hills and a lot of people want to take the Black Hills from the Indians, but wouldn't you know it, the Indians don't want to give them up. Course the Indians will be chased out—eventually. They've always been chased out of anywhere settlers want to go. Right now the Hills belong to the Indians, and they are defending them as best they can. Officially, the army is also supposed to keep settlers and prospectors out of there. So this is slowing things down, and gives us a chance to get in there before everything is claimed up."

Karl was a little perplexed. "Get in there! How do you get in there when the Indians and army are trying to keep you out?"

"It's not like nobody is getting in," Pat explained. "Here's what I have been told and have read about in the Chicago paper. Prospectors and settlers are moving into some of the valleys in the northern hills where the best gold prospects are, and they intend to stay. The valleys can be defended against Indians pretty easily, and the army won't come in and slaughter a bunch of citizens. The trick is to get to those settlements. There are four trails you can take to get there. They all go through Indian territory. The Indians hang back and pick you off if they can, but if you are with a large enough group, they won't bother you."

The more Karl was finding out about the scheme, the wilder it was sounding. "Heinrich, I can't believe you are going along with this wild idea!" he exclaimed.

Heinrich defended the plan. "There are regular trains of wagons hauling supplies on those trails. A bunch of supply haulers and anyone that wants to go with them form a group, and if it's big enough they don't have any trouble. Once you get to the settlements, things are pretty safe."

Pat had it all figured out. "We take the Chicago and Northwestern train from Chicago to Council Bluffs in Iowa, then get on the Union Pacific and ride it to Sidney, Nebraska. There we hook up with a supply train and take the Sidney trail to Deadwood. Takes about two-three weeks on the trail, and then we are there."

The word Nebraska perked Karl's attention. It reminded him of his early intent to make it to Omaha and work toward his goal of homesteading from there. Many things and much time had intervened between then and his meeting today with Pat and Heinrich, but it certainly struck a familiar chord.

Pat continued, "We are going to do it, Heinrich and me. We will be out of here by the end of May. We'll head for Chicago, stock up there with what we think we will need and head out sometime in June. We would like to have you along, Karl. You would add weight to the party. We could use a steady partner like you."

Karl couldn't tell if they were sincere in their compliments, or just buttering him up, appealing to his vanity in order to get him to join them. In either case, he was not overwhelmed by the prospects of the adventure the two were contemplating.

"What do you hope to get out of this?" Karl asked. "It sounds like a lot of risk and a lot of not knowing what you are doing."

Karl suspected that Heinrich and Pat probably did not have a good answer for his question. A young man's itch for adventure might have been the honest answer, but Heinrich came up with something that sounded reasonable.

"Money. Gold. You have to take chances to get real money. A dollar a day will keep you poor if you do that the rest of your life."

Karl had to agree with what Heinrich was saying, but not with the means they were planning to use. "It sounds like you are hoping to find a pot of money out there. The odds of that happening are not good."

There was more back-and- forth talk, and Karl listened to their arguments, but finally he raised his glass and proclaimed, "Have a good trip. I'm going to find me some land and settle down."

Heinrich and Pat were disappointed, but they understood.

When they departed that evening, Karl was certain of his plans. They had not changed. He was not going to be diverted by the wild adventure that Heinrich and Pat were contemplating. Yet Karl could not get the Black Hills completely out of his mind. Karl did not believe instant riches were likely. That was something that happened in fairy stories, not real life. The magnet that was drawing Karl was curiosity, adventure. It was west, the direction that he expected to go. He had been focusing on eastern Dakota which was wide open and where good farm land could be found. He had heard that western Dakota was too arid for ordinary farming, and besides, it was an Indian reservation. But still, those Black Hills intrigued him.

A sudden turn of events gave Karl an excuse to re-examine his decision. In what was to be Pat's last week in the mill, there was an accident. This was not unusual. It was the type of accident that occurred frequently in the mills. Pat got his left hand in the way of a circular saw. It sliced off his small and ring fingers and about a quarter of the hand below the fingers. He could have lost the whole hand very easily, it was a matter of an inch one way or the other.

The Northwest company had a procedure for handling accidents since they occurred frequently. It had arranged to refer any accident cases to a two-doctor office. The company paid the doctors for any first aid and for an assessment of the injury. If the injury was disabling and the worker would not be able to continue in his line of work after recovering, the person was terminated and would have to take care of any additional medical bills himself. However, if the injury was not disabling and the worker could return to his job after recovering and was considered a good credit risk, the company would lend the worker money for his medical care and living expenses. These loans were to be paid back out of future wages to be earned working for the company. Interest at the market rate was charged. The arrangement had mutual benefits. The company kept a trained employee and the expenses incurred were paid back with interest. The employee was able to pay his bills while he was recovering and was assured of a job once he was ready to return to work. Pat qualified for the return-to-work plan and he needed and appreciated the company assistance. But would tie him to the company for many years and therefore eliminated any plans to join Heinrich in the Black Hills gold rush. Pat wasn't happy about the state of affairs, but as he put it, "Life is a bitch. We have to play with the hand it deals us."

Heinrich was devastated. He did not feel comfortable joining the gold rush on his own, but he still had a strong desire to make the journey. He appealed to Karl once more. The adventurous and irresponsible part of Karl's subconscious used the accident as a reason to agree that he would go in Pat's place.

# CHAPTER 21

▼

# THE SIDNEY LAYOVER

The first leg of the journey to Deadwood was from Eau Claire to Chicago by train.

When they arrived in Chicago, Karl searched out his bank on LaSalle Street. He took a hundred dollars of the money he had earned as a lumberjack and added it to the hundred dollars, plus eight dollars earned interest, already in his savings account. The remainder of his lumberjack earnings would be used to finance the Black Hills adventure. Hopefully, he would add to his savings during the Black Hills diversion. Enough to allow him to finally reach his goal.

Karl and Heinrich shopped for supplies they believed they would need for the journey. Extra clothes, bedding, a tent, and a revolver for each of them. Being armed was not optional when traveling in Indian country, and it was rumored that carrying a gun was *de rigeur* in Deadwood.

They packed up and boarded a Chicago and Northwestern train that was headed for Council Bluffs, Iowa, on June 24, 1876. In Council Bluffs they would switch to the new transcontinental Union Pacific for the final leg to Sidney, Nebraska. They left Chicago mid-afternoon and traveled through flat Illinois farmland dotted with neat farmsteads and thriving crops. It was an agricultural panorama that bored many of the passengers, but held Karl transfixed. Karl realized that each one of those farmsteads represented an enterprising farmer and a family that most likely owned it. They worked the land and cared for the livestock for their own benefit, not for a baron or a lord. This was a tangible sample of what he was striving to achieve.

By evening they had reached the Mississippi River and crossed it—on a bridge that must have been a mile long—and entered Iowa. They traveled all night through the state of Iowa and the next morning still had a ways to go before reaching its western border. The scenery had changed. They were now traveling through prairie with farmsteads here and there. This was country just being settled; this is what Karl was looking for. He liked what he saw. A lot of low, marshy land, but plenty of rolling hills covered with tall grass, waiting to be plowed and made into crop-land. At Council Bluffs, Iowa, they switched to the Union Pacific and crossed the wide Missouri on what appeared to be a brand-new bridge into Omaha. Omaha, the place that was Karl's original destination five years ago. It looked like a thriving river town, but certainly was not a Chicago.

As they proceeded into Nebraska, the tracks followed the flat Platte River valley, so broad that the extent of it could not be discerned from the train. For a short distance west of Omaha, much of the land was settled and had been converted from grass to crop land. As they proceeded, the grass remained lush and green, but there were few settlers. Karl mused, "Still a lot of room for more settlers." The grass grew shorter further west. Here conditions and climate appeared to support cattle grazing rather than crop farming. Karl and Heinrich had heard about the abundant buffalo on the western prairies and looked forward to seeing them, but were disappointed. Other passengers told them they were a continuous presence when the track was laid ten years previously, but were now a curiosity and seldom seen.

Night fell as they continued the journey westward. The dawn of a new day found the valley had narrowed, and low rolling hills flanking the valley were visible from either side of the train. By mid-morning, they had arrived in Sidney.

The scenery was in sharp contrast to the northern woods of Wisconsin. The hills at the edge of the valley were treeless, covered with short grass and sage brush. The town seemed to consist of buildings built about ten years ago with a life expectancy of about ten years. So, despite the town's short history, it looked run down. An exception was a clutch of buildings to the east of the town's center that appeared to be well maintained. They were told that was Fort Sidney, an army outpost.

The streets consisted mostly of fine sand, which frequent winds would blow around in eye-watering gusts. The sun came up bright and early that time of the year, and the treeless town soon become relentlessly hot.

It did not look like a good place to spend a lot of time. The two men found that the next wagon train would be leaving for Deadwood in four days. That wouldn't be too soon.

Accommodations were limited, as expected, and they put the tent they carried with them to good use. Karl and Heinrich found out about wagon train procedures and costs. They would haul your gear for eight cents a pound and for fifteen dollars you got the privilege of walking along. Food was supplied. For forty dollars they would haul and feed you.

"Sounds kind of high to me," opined Heinrich. "Fare from Chicago was only ten dollars, and we got to ride."

"You want to get out of Sidney, you have to pay the price."

"Ya, it might be worth it."

✳   ✳   ✳   ✳

Shortly after arriving in Sidney they heard news of army debacles to the north. General Crook had made a strategic retreat from Rosebud.(Interpretation: Got his ass out of there before he got creamed). General Custer, in the process of teaching the Indians some manners, had gotten his troops and himself massacred. Karl and Heinrich did not understand the full impact of these developments, but from the way the news was greeted by locals and people who understood those kinds of things, it was apparently ominous for anyone planning to go to the Black Hills.

Some of the people waiting for the next wagon train to Deadwood changed their plans. For them, apparently the fear of the Indians was mightier than the lure of gold.

Heinrich asked Karl what he thought about the situation.

Karl was concerned, but didn't consider the news inconsistent with what they were expecting. "Pat said the Indians would be trying to keep prospectors out of the hills, and that seems to be what they are doing."

The news from up north caused enough concern to delay the planned departure of the wagon train until the middle of the following week. They were trying to add to the number of people that would be traveling with the wagon train. Actually the delay may have aggravated the problem because a double wagon rig with a dozen pairs of oxen and six men threatened to take off on their own if the original schedule was not kept. The wagon master was undeterred. He stuck with the revised schedule and told the renegades that it would be crazy to take off by themselves. A man named Shorty ran the breakaway wagons. He was an impatient man. He had not seen an Indian on the two previous trips they had made this spring and he was not worried. Shorty, his wagons, and six men took off on the originally scheduled departure date.

There were not a lot of diversions in Sidney for anyone waiting for a wagon train to leave. There were a few raunchy saloons that catered to the wagon train crowd, railroad workers, and army men on a pass, a few prostitutes, and not much else.

Heinrich occasionally played poker with some of the other men waiting for the wagon train departure. Locals would sometimes join them. Karl, always reluctant to put any of his hard-earned money into play, only watched. Heinrich enjoyed playing the game, but was careful to limit the amount he would put at risk and normally stayed pretty close to even.

One night Heinrich was having a pretty good streak and was ahead of the game. It was five-card draw and the pot was being bid up on this particular deal. By the time it got around to Heinrich, he had to put most of his winnings in to stay, but he had two red aces and felt compelled to see what he would draw. He drew a black ace and a pair of jacks—full house, aces high. He maintained an admirably calm poker face. The first bidder called, and the next one pushed his whole pile in. This fellow was new in town. Maybe he thought he could bluff the locals. His raise added up to twenty dollars. Heinrich felt a little faint. If the guy was bluffing he was doing a real good job of it. Heinrich had never played with stakes this high. But his cards were close to being the best possible hand in the game. He turned to Karl. "Loan me five."

"Are you crazy?" Karl replied, but he reached into his pocket and pulled out gold and silver equaling five dollars.

Heinrich reached under his shirt and came up with twenty dollars, just about all the money he had and what he needed to get to Deadwood. He put the twenty and the five he borrowed from Karl on the table. "See you and raise you five."

It would cost twenty-five dollars to stay in. That, plus what was already in the pot, added up to thirty dollars for each player. Everyone dropped except the new fellow from out of town and a local. The local pulled his stack out of the pot, then wrote something on a piece of paper and put it into the pot.

"That's a yoke of oxen," the local said. "That's my call, a yoke of oxen."

The new guy protested, "Only real money, no animals or chickens. Who knows what that yoke is worth?"

The local defended his bid. "That yoke is worth more than thirty dollars, lots more, twice as much. Ask anyone that knows around here."

Heinrich was somewhat familiar with what oxen were worth, and thirty dollars sounded like a good value, if they were healthy animals. "What kind of shape are those animals in?" Heinrich asked.

"They are five years old, in their prime."

"I'll take a chance on them," Heinrich pronounced. "Anyone else want to see the cards?"

The stranger said he would write an IOU.

"Real money," Heinrich instructed. "Or oxen."

The stranger was incensed, started ranting about what a bullshit small-time game this was, then threw down his cards.

The local looked at Heinrich. "Let's see 'em."

Heinrich showed his full house and the game was over.

"What are you going to do with a yoke of oxen?" Karl was asking the obvious when the game ended.

"Haul me to Deadwood," replied Heinrich.

"Haul you in what?"

"Small problem," Heinrich assured him.

However, the conveyance to go with the oxen turned out to be a bigger problem than Heinrich anticipated. A good wagon, any wagon, was a scarce item in western Nebraska and expensive if one could be found. A dealer in Sidney had a couple of wagons, but they were in bad condition, and their ability to hold together on the trail to Deadwood was doubtful. They had loose rims, missing spokes, and rotted boxes. While searching for wagons, Heinrich spotted an object laying among other debris in an equipment dealer's yard. It was about ten feet long and three wide, with a plank bed and two sturdy oak logs running the full length on the bottom. A log chain was attached to one end, apparently to pull the object.

Heinrich pointed to it. "What's that?" he asked.

"Stone-boat. Use it to haul rocks out of fields."

Karl looked at Heinrich. "I hope you aren't thinking what I think you are thinking," he remarked, while eyeing Heinrich suspiciously.

"Why not? We could strap our stuff on there and ride or walk along side."

"How much?" Heinrich asked the dealer.

"Three dollars."

"With the chain?"

"Another half dollar for the chain."

So Heinrich and Karl ended up with an unlikely conveyance for the journey to Deadwood. Two oxen and a stone-boat. They made minor modifications to the stone-boat, adding foot-high plank sides and front to it, and laid a plank across the sideboards to form a seat. With the added features, their baggage and supplies would stay put and they would have a place to sit if they got tired of walking. Even Karl had to admit that it had turned out better than he had expected.

Under normal conditions, the wagon train boss might not have been interested in having such a contraption in his caravan, but conditions weren't normal and he was ready to take anything that was willing to go. For twenty five dollars, the normal wagon fee, he would let them join the group.

Now with a platform to haul things, they added items to their provisions, including mining picks and shovels. They even agreed to haul gear for one of the walkers for three dollars.

A man waiting for the wagon train to leave had second thoughts about his plans and decided to head back east where he had come from. The man was in his fifties, a little overweight, and wore back east cloths. He was not comfortable on the frontier, and the Indian situation added to his discomfort. Prior to leaving, the man put up for sale items that he would no longer need. Included in those items was a Winchester .44 lever action rifle.

Karl saw the rifle as an opportunity to relieve a worry he had after hearing about the increased Indian threat. He was concerned that they were only carrying revolvers. He explained to Heinrich, "With revolvers you have to be close to what you are shooting at, which can be dangerous if what you are shooting at can shoot back." Karl suggested that the rifle would be a good place for Heinrich to invest some of his poker winnings. Karl would pay his share out of the first gold he dug up in Deadwood.

Heinrich was all for it, except he wanted to know how Karl would pay if they didn't find any gold.

"You have doubts?" Karl asked incredulously.

The man wanted twenty dollars for the rifle. Since rifles were a high demand item, they didn't haggle, and paid him his asking price.

Despite the week's delay, the wagon master still didn't have the number of people he would have liked for his wagon train. However he didn't want to delay the departure any longer. The freight haulers didn't make money idling in Sidney—they needed to get moving.

Before departing, the wagon master assembled the people that would be traveling with him. He was a veteran of the Civil and Indian wars who, at the urging of his wife who was not fond of living on the frontier, had retired early with the permanent rank of captain; This past winter he had been lured back west by an attractive offer to run wagon trains to the Black Hills. He was a tall man with a commanding presence. He climbed up on the wheel of one of the wagons and addressed the group.

He made it clear that he as wagon master would be in command of the group while they were underway. He would decide when they would be moving out in the morning and where and when they would be putting up for the night. He would assign members of the group to tasks needing to be done each day: preparing meals, cleaning up, performing sentry duty. In any emergency situation, the wagon master would be in charge. his decisions and his orders were to be followed without hesitation. This is how things would be done. These were the rules and if anyone felt that they could not work with them, they should consider finding a different way of getting to Deadwood.

Finally he asked, "Any questions?"

There were none.

When they departed the next morning, there were four double freight wagon rigs with a dozen yoke of oxen pulling each and one three freight wagon rig with eighteen yokes of oxen pulling it. The freight wagons were all hauling general cargo. They figured about a thousand pounds of weight for each yoke of oxen, so the wagon train was hauling approximately twenty tons of cargo to be delivered to Deadwood. The freight wagons used heavy wagon running gear with wood-spoked wheels as high as a tall man with steel rims a foot wide. The freight wagon boxes were improvised using heavy planks and designed to maximize the number of cubic feet available to haul cargo. Each wagon was covered with a heavy canvas to protect the cargo from the weather. There were no seats on the cargo wagons and the bull whackers and their assistants walked along side the oxen. There were five prairie schooners in the caravan. Each had the traditional schooner box and hoops with canvas stretched over it to protect the people or the cargo in the wagon. There was a seldom-used seat for the driver. One of the schooners was hauling three female passengers, one five-year-old child, and the passenger's baggage. The other four schooners carried walker and crew baggage, food and other supplies needed for the trip, and general cargo in any left over space. A yoke of oxen pulled each prairie schooner.

One bull whacker and two assistants were assigned to each freight rig, and there was one driver with each prairie schooner. The rest of the caravan included the wagon master, Heinrich and his oxen, Karl, ten other walkers, and six horsemen, for a total of thirty-eight men, all well armed. They made a formidable presence on the prairie, but not up to the desirable minimum of fifty men for a wagon train going through Indian territory.

# CHAPTER 22

▼

# ON THE SIDNEY TO DEADWOOD TRAIL

The caravan set off over the rolling Nebraska sand hills before daybreak. The horsemen took turns acting as outriders, a pair of them ranging a mile or two ahead of the train as it plodded through the hills. Short dry grass crackled under the feet of the men and animals as they headed straight north on the Sidney to Deadwood trail. The terrain was rolling, and despite the summer heat and drought there were small ponds of water in low places between the hills. The ponds were edged with rushes and a few water fowl paddled about, offering visual relief to the otherwise arid land. The heat built up relentlessly as the day progressed and the sun climbed higher in the sky.

"Not farming country," Karl assured Heinrich. "Too dry to raise crops. You could graze cattle, but would need more than a hundred and sixty acres, a lot more."

Heinrich thought less of its potential. "I would say this country is not much good for anything except for getting somewhere else."

At around ten o'clock in the morning the wagon train halted near a large pond. They unhooked the animals, let them drink from the pond, and then let them graze on the dry but plentiful grass. It was time for the oxen to replenish their energy. Oxen were able to live off the land, but it took time, and the wagon train had to halt and patiently wait for them to graze and digest their meal.

While the oxen browsed, the wagon train members also had their big meal of the day. Everything needed was carried in the wagons, including fuel for fires since the trail was largely treeless. Wagon train members designated as cooks prepared the meal, which consisted of beans, rice, hardtack, and salted pork. There were dried apples for dessert, and honey that Heinrich drizzled over hardtack. There were large pots of coffee and tea.

The cooks told them to get used to it. This, with minor variations, would be the menu for the rest of the trip. Food would be plain, but plentiful. The wagon master took advantage of the meal gathering to hand out the next day's assignments to the men who would serve as sentries, cooks, and herders.

After the meal, Karl and Heinrich relaxed and smoked their pipes. Karl even dozed for awhile.

At about three o'clock the animals were assembled into their pulling stations, and within an hour the wagon train was again underway.

In the early evening, a few thunder heads floated in from the west. One dropped a cooling sprinkle and a lot of lightning that scared the horses but didn't seem to faze the oxen. They kept going until they had reached a planned stopping point at eight thirty. The days were long that time of the year, and there was enough daylight to get the wagon train ready for the night. Although they weren't yet into Indian territory, the wagons were arranged in a protective circle, a practice that would be followed for the rest of the trip. The oxen were turned loose to browse on the grass growing around the site, watched by the designated herders, while the horses were kept tethered. Oxen were not likely to go anywhere fast, while the horses could be long gone if spooked. The horse's diet was supplemented with oats, while the oxen could do just fine on the grass they browsed.

The evening meal was a repetition of the noon meal, but more hurried because the wagon train members were tired and ready to get some rest. It wasn't long before the only signs of life were the smoldering fires and designated sentries moving about the camp.

It was still dark when a sentry started banging on an iron pot. "Everybody up, reveille, let's get going."

Breakfast was a rerun of the previous day's meals.

The animals were assembled and the wagon train was on its way. The previous day they had made ten miles. Today they expected to make a little more than that. That was average milage for a wagon train.

Six days into the journey, right after pausing for the mid-day break, one of the outriders rode up to the wagon master.

"Herd of buffalo on the other side of that ridge. Must be a hundred, maybe more."

"How far?"

"About a mile."

"We got any buffalo hunters here?"

"I've hunted buffalo."

"What you think the chances are of getting some buffalo meat?"

"If we had horses trained to hunt it would be a cinch. But the best chance might be to take half a dozen men and sneak up on the windward side of that ridge. Then have a couple of men on horses ride up the draw, try to drive them towards the men waiting to ambush them."

The wagon master liked the idea. "Pick a crew and get us fresh meat. If I hear you shooting, I'll send up a wagon to fetch what you have."

The buffalo hunter picked five men besides himself to set the trap. Karl was one of them. Although they weren't visible, this was as close as Karl had been to buffalo since coming out west. He had heard much about them and their abundance, but certainly they were not abundant along the route they had been traveling. This would also be a chance to try out the Winchester lever action, a good buffalo gun.

The hunting party moved out on foot at a quick pace, hoping the buffalo would stay put long enough for them to carry out the planned maneuver. It was easy walking; there were no obstacles. The only vegetation was short prairie grass and scrubby sage with a dusky scent. The ground was flat with only occasional shallow washouts from heavy rains. They moved across the baked prairie to a point where they could start up the slope to the ridge where they hoped to ambush the buffalo.

Before starting up the slope, the buffalo hunter gave them their final instructions. "When we get a couple hundred feet short of the ridge, we will spread out about twenty feet apart. Then stay put while I go up to the ridge to see where the buffalo are. I'll wave the rest of you to move up if things look good. You move up, move slow, crawl the last fifty feet or so, keep your spacing. When you get to the ridge, don't show anything you don't have to. The horsemen will be driving them towards us. Try to pick an animal directly in front of you. Don't want everyone shooting the same animal. Young cow if you can, best meat. I will take the first shot, then start shooting."

They moved up the slope until the leader indicated they had gone far enough. The hunters spread out and the leader started to move up the final distance to the ridge. As they waited, Karl sat down beside a sage plant and studied some ants busily working around its base. He noticed that what he always labeled grass was really a variety of plants thickly intertwined together. It would be interesting to know what all those plants were called. In any case, it was a lot of good browse for buffalo or cattle. His reverie was interrupted when the leader, who had gained the ridge, motioned for the others to move up the slope.

Karl crouched down, moved up most way and then crawled when he got near to the top of the ridge. The herd came into view when he reached the crest of the ridge. Finally, he was seeing the famous buffalo, and they were within rifle range. They were close enough that he could hear an occasional snort. The horsemen were still some distance off, but the herd was starting to move towards them. Young calves hung on the sides of their browsing mothers. A bull would occasionally lift its head and sniff the air. There were signs of concern caused by the approaching horsemen, but no panic.

They were magnificent specimens. The enlarged front quarter canted the animal such that it appeared to be in a state of perpetual ascendance. Their brown coats were patchy as a result of shedding in the summer heat, but it didn't hide the lithe, muscular bodies. They were larger and more impressive than Karl had imagined they would be.

Karl selected what he believed to be a young cow, an easy big target, and waited for the leader to fire. A shot rang out, followed by a volley of shoots, followed by sporadic shooting. Karl's cow gave a jump with the first shot he fired. He levered another shell into the chamber and fired again and the animal sank to knees, and then fell on its side.

A large bull in the herd gave a snort and a confused bawl. There was a threat in the form of horsemen coming towards them, but there also seemed to be other danger coming from an uncertain direction. The herd reacted to the known threat and charged directly toward the ambushing riflemen. Karl stood up to face the charging herd. He was no longer interested in killing buffalo, only in getting out of their way. A hundred charging animals is a formidable sight, but the numbers were not numerous enough to be a solid mass and there were gaps and enough visibility for man and animal to avoid colliding. The herd ran through the hunters without inflicting any damage.

Eight animals were left behind, downed by the ambushing riflemen. The hunters took out their knifes and started working on the animals. Most were experienced at butchering, and those that weren't learned on the job. They were only interested in the prime meat on the back side, so the animals were rolled with their legs under them and a slit was made down the back and the hide was peeled out and down. The cows weren't as big as bulls, but they were still huge, ten feet long from head to tail. The boss, the hump just behind the nap of the neck, was sliced off. Then the men worked on the prime pieces. Thin flesh covering the ribs, called the fleece, was peeled off. The tenderloin, the side ribs, and the tongue were removed from the animals. There were still two animals left to butcher when the wagon sent by the wagon master arrived to load the meat. They had more than enough meat by that time, so they took only the humps and tongues off those last two carcasses.

The cook crew had the fires burning when the wagon with the meat arrived back at the campsite. Some green willow saplings cut from the banks of a nearby pond were sharpened, pointed, and readied for use as meat skewers. The meat was laid out on bloody buffalo hides, and cut into steaks, roasts, and ribs. The steaks with alternating strips of fine fleece were jammed onto the green wood stakes which were propped up to hold meat over the blazing fire. The tenderloins and slabs of ribs were roasted in one piece in the same manner. The air was soon filled with the savory smell of roasting buffalo meat, watched over hungrily by the wagon train members who had not tasted fresh meat for many days. As soon as the meat, drizzling with fleece fat, turned brown, it was pulled from the fire, and the wagon train members began gorging themselves. The three women in the wagon train made a pass at being dainty, using plates, utensils, and carving knives, but the majority of the men used their bare hands to eat the savory meat.

Heinrich and Karl each took a large steak dripping with fat in their hands, and after tasting it, Heinrich had to admit it was some of the tastiest meat he had ever chewed. They were soon eating lustily in the manner demonstrated by the other diners. Grease was running down both sides of their faces and chins. Karl encouraged Heinrich to eat hearty. "We have enough meat for a couple of armies so you don't need to hold back."

Heinrich didn't.

After downing the steaks they tackled some sizzling ribs.

As Heinrich sucked the marrow out of a rib, he said he was beginning to understand why the Indians worshiped the buffalo.

Karl asked, "Do they worship them? How do you know that?"

"A bull whacker told me. If they don't, they should."

Every man and woman ate until they were sated and there were groans, grunts, and sighs, a mixture of pleasure and pain. Water was heated and tea and coffee were made. Tin cups were filled and the wagon train members relaxed and enjoyed sipping the hot beverages. It was unusually quiet for a while, but conversations finally emerged from the mellow group.

One of the wagon train veterans started talking about buffalo.

"Seeing a herd of buffalo these days is like a big event," a grizzled bull whacker was saying, "Damn, it wasn't over ten years ago, they were so thick you could hardly drive oxen across the plains."

The wagon master recalled shooting buffalo in the old days. "You didn't have to sneak up on them, you could shoot them right off the wagon. You were hardly ever out of sight of buffalo."

"Where did they all go?" Karl wanted to know.

The wagon master, who had served in the army, gave his version of the reason for their disappearance. "The army figured the buffalo was the Indian's quartermaster. Get rid of the buffalo and you could control the Indians. The ranchers and farmers didn't want them running over the land either, but I never believed they could get rid of them, there were so many. It is hard to believe that they have almost disappeared."

Karl didn't feel he was qualified to talk buffalo with this crowd, but he felt compelled to voice some reservations about their hunt.

"You know, it bothered me a little that we just ate some of the best meat off those animals and left tons of meat to rot. I worked in a butcher shop, packing plant, and we killed a lot of animals, but we used everything."

"The Indians, the same way," a grizzled bull whacker testified. "They use everything."

Another veteran put his oar in. "Don't worry about that meat rotting. The vultures, wolves, coyotes will have it cleaned up soon enough."

That night they ate buffalo meat again, and again the following morning. It would not keep much longer in the summer heat, so what hadn't been eaten by then was left for the coyotes.

It was a welcome, if short, respite from the standard fare.

\*        \*        \*        \*

The Sidney trail skirted the east side of the Black Hills, and they were soon on the edge of low hills that formed a picket line for pine and spruce-covered higher hills and mountains barely visible on the horizon.

The wagon master pointed out the hills to Karl. "See those further hills? What color would you say they were?"

Karl looked closely. The brown foreground simmered under the high sun, while on the horizon, where the hills stood taller, there seemed to be a dark border outlining the landscape spread before them. "They look dark in this bright light."

"Now you know why the Indians call them the Black Hills."

"I was wondering about that."

The wagon master was happy to see those hills. It was a sure sign that the wagon train was making progress towards its destination.

It was about this time Heinrich voiced some concern about their stone boat. "Those runners are about half worn off. At this rate the thing will fall apart before we get to where we are going."

Karl agreed. "This gritty ground is like a scraper. Probably don't help to be hauling old Ben either."

They had been hauling one walker about half time. He had sore feet and didn't have the money to pay the wagon train forty dollars to ride, so he paid five dollars to ride part-time on the stone boat.

Heinrich didn't think the extra weight made much difference. "If we were pulling it empty it would still wear down. Like you said, the sand is the problem."

Karl agreed. "You are probably right. It's not hard to figure out what we need to fix it—new runners and some hardware to fasten it together. The hard part is to figure out where in hell you get those things in the middle of Indian country."

One of the bull whackers noted signs of Indians along the trail, something that hadn't been seen in earlier trips.

The wagon master told everyone to be alert. "The Indians have been busy with Generals Crook and Custer. Now that the army is pretty much out of commission, maybe they are going to start to work on the trails. If they could take on General Custer and a couple hundred of the best army troops, they wouldn't have much trouble with a wagon train."

The day the Black Hills were sighted, the wagon train prepared for its mid-day break in high spirits. They still had a ways to go but now had tangible evidence of progress towards their destination.

The wagons were drawn into the customary circle, the oxen were put out to graze, and five of the horses in the train were also picketed near the oxen to partake of some particularly good grass. Two sentries/herders watched over the grazing oxen and picketed horses while the rest of the crew prepared for their midday meal. The campsite was on a small rise, with a relatively large drop-off towards the west that sloped towards a creek with a scattering of trees lining it. There was also a series of deep gullies cut into the bank leading to the creek. One of the herders was on horseback, lolling on the far side of the oxen herd. Another herder was on foot between the herd and the drop-off. The horses were picketed near the herder on foot.

The wagon train members were eating when several whoops and loud bangs like gun shots were heard.

There was a pause in the eating and a sentry standing near the edge of the circled wagons gave a shout.

"The horses are being chased off!"

The horse owners were immediately on their feet and started running towards where the horses had been picketed. Others joined them. Some had guns, some didn't. It was soon obvious that the horses were being driven off by mounted Indians in the direction of the drop-off. The wagon train members were all on foot and had no chance of saving the horses. The wagon master took control of the situation. He was shouting, "Everybody get your guns if you don't have them, then fall in over here where I am. Everybody!"

The men getting armed were back in minutes, but by that time the Indians had disappeared over the ridge. The wagon train could be under attack at any minute.

The wagon master gave a series of orders. "I will take all the walkers and horsemen out to find the sentries and look for Indians. Heinrich, that includes you. Bull whackers, wagon drivers, bring the animals into the circle. The rest of the men stay with the wagons and cover those going out."

Karl realized that the wagon train was in a precarious position. A large portion of the fighting strength of the wagon train was committed to the risky task of reconnoitering for unfriendly Indians, locating the sentries, and retrieving the oxen. It was an aggressive move that would at least determine the Indian's intent. If the intent was to attack the wagon train, they would soon be engaged. If the Indians were only interested in the horses, that would soon be known.

The walkers and horsemen, including Karl and Heinrich moved away from the protection of the circled wagons and towards the drop-off where the Indians had disappeared. The wagon master had them spread out at intervals of about twenty feet.

As the men moved toward the ridge and gullies that could be filled with unfriendly Indians, Karl felt a grip of fear similar to what he had experienced before in battle. He concentrated on the man ahead of him and the surrounding terrain. He cocked the Winchester rifle and held it in a ready position.

They came upon the sentry who had been on foot near the drop off. Bill, shot dead and scalped. The wagon master cautiously approached the edge of the drop-off where the land fell away towards the creek where they had watered the animals earlier in the day. When he got to where he could look over the edge, he signaled the other men to join him.

The wagon master pointed to a cloud of dust in the distance where a number of horsemen were driving other unmounted horses before them. "There go our horses. Looks like it was a small party after our horses."

A bull whacker ran up. They had found the second sentry. Killed and scalped.

The wagon master directed his group to do a thorough search of the ridge and gullies for Indians.

There was no sign of Indians in the gullies. The worst of the crisis was over.

They retrieved the bodies of the sentries and moved the oxen into the circle. There was a feeling of relief when the animals and all of the wagon train members were back within the perimeter. They were now in a position of strength relative to their numbers.

The wagon master directed the men to finish their dinner and then gathered everyone to lay out the plans for the rest of the day. First, he assessed the situation. It wasn't good, but he put as good a face on it as he could. "We've been hurt, lost two good men. All of the horses are gone. But we are still 36 men, about that many rifles, lots of hand guns. It would take a large party of Sioux to overwhelm us. It looks like it was a small party that took the horses. But we can't assume this the end of it."

The concern of the wagon train members showed in their grime faces. The risk they had assumed to get to gold fields of the Black Hills was now being played out. The under-maned wagon train was in the middle of hostel Indian territory. They had sustained an Indian attack and were threatened by further attacks.

"What now Captain?" A bush whacker asked.

"We will move out as soon as we can get organized. Tonight we will bypass the place we planned to camp, go to another place a couple of hours further on. If they have any plans for us in the morning, that should confuse them. They won't attack at night, early morning is their favorite time. Hopefully they won't know where we are spending the night. In the future we will double the guard when the oxen are grazing."

There was buzz from the group, "Think we can travel at night?"

"The trail is well marked. Shouldn't be a problem. From now on we will be pushing as hard as the oxen can be driven. This trail is not a good place to be right now."

Someone suggested that they pray a lot.

"For those so inclined." The wagon master replied.

If anyone questioned the plans outlined, they kept them to themselves. The wagon master's job was to make these decisions. The wagon train members had accepted that when they signed on.

The bodies of the two slain men would be carried with them and buried at the next camp site.

If the oxen were perplexed by the extended work day, it wasn't apparent. They plodded without complaint along the dark trail until camp was finally made in the middle of the night.

Despite the short night, the wagon train was underway on schedule the next morning, now more vigilant and more aware of the danger that lurked just out of sight.

While walking the trail, Heinrich revealed to Karl some of his concerns about his reaction to the previous days events.

"When we went toward that ridge, I was scared as hell."

"You did walk out there."

"Ya, I did. Didn't want to look like a coward."

"Everyone is scared when their life is threatened. The army told us that's how your body gets itself ready for danger. It's alert as it can get when scared. So the army wants you to be scared, but they train you to be more scared of looking like a coward than getting killed."

"When you think about it, that don't make a lot of sense."

"That's the other thing the army teaches you—not to think."

Later that day, when it was nearing the time for the mid-day break, vultures were seen circling off to the left side of the trail. There was something laying on the ground that was attracting them, but it wasn't possible to make out what it was from the trail. One of the walkers decided to have a closer look and trotted towards the objects. When he got close, he stopped, hesitated, turned, and hurried back to the wagon train. Out of breath, he gasped, "Dead people, a bunch of em."

The wagon master organized a party to investigate further. Karl was part of the party.

They could smell the dead bodies before they became fully visible.

When they got close, one of the party started retching. Karl stifled the same sensation.

There were four putrefied bodies, half consumed by vultures, covered with flies, and maggots. Although it was hard to tell for sure, they probably had been scalped.

Even in their deteriorated state, the wagon master was able to identify them. "It's the Shorty Williams crew. Shorty never wanted to wait for anyone. Won't have to wait anymore. There were six of them, should be two more someplace."

"Them red devils are like wolves, pick off the weak ones," remarked one of the men.

The wagon master seemed angry. "Why in the hell not? They were like ripe fruit. It was suicide to go through with a single wagon. Suicide."

The wagon train paused to bury the four bodies and search for the other two. They did not find the missing men, but did find the wagons in a little draw. The cargo was picked over and the wagons had been burned.

Karl noted that the wagons had burned, but the heavy oak tongues on both wagons were only singed. It occurred to him that this was the solution to their stone-boat problem.

The wagon master agreed that Karl could salvage whatever he wanted from the remains, but must be ready to move as soon as the burial of Shorty and his crew was completed.

Karl and Heinrich borrowed some tools from the wagon train tool box, removed the two wagon tongues, then cut them in half.

Ben joined them and scrounged for hardware. The Indians were not looking for screws, nuts, and bolts when they went through the cargo, and Ben soon had a large assortment of hardware that he collected in a wooden box. When he had the box about half full he called to Heinrich and Karl, "Got enough spikes, bolts, and screws to hold a couple of stone-boats together."

Karl looked them over. "That's for sure. Load 'em up."

The tongues that had been cut in half were also loaded onto the stone-boat, and they rejoined the wagon train as it prepared to move on. This was not a good place to linger.

The wagon train progressed another couple of miles before pausing for the mid-day break. After the camp was set up, Karl, Heinrich, and Ben put new runners on the stone-boat.

The tongues that had been cut in half were bolted together into two pairs of runners, each about six inches high, eight inches wide, and ten feet long.

Heinrich was satisfied with the results. "Should get us the rest of the way."

Ben figured it could get them to Oregon if they wanted to go that far.

The wagon train pressed on, pushing the oxen as hard as the wagon master felt possible. Members of the wagon train would often see Indians in the distance shadowing the column of wagons. Everyone knew that the Indians were over the horizon, or behind those hills, and that at anytime they could be fighting for their lives. The wagon caravan's presence had shrunk; its outriders had been lost with the horses, and the wagons stayed close together for mutual protection. The playfulness sometimes displayed during the first part of the journey had largely disappeared.

As they approached Rapid City, spirits began to rise.

"If them red devils are going to get us, they better hurry," a bull whacker opined. "Never heard of a train having problems once they get past Rapid City."

There was a genuine feeling of relief when the wagon train finally trundled into Rapid City, a relief further reinforced when they merged with another wagon train coming from Fort Pierre, more than doubling the size of the caravan.

In three more days they reached the entrance to the narrow valley where a gold flecked stream ran and where Deadwood lay. The wagon train had run the Sidney to Deadwood gauntlet, and when they rolled through the streets of Deadwood, it set off a minor celebration, as did every wagon train that arrived that summer.

# CHAPTER 23

▼

# DEADWOOD, 1876

Chaos might be the best word to describe what Karl and Heinrich observed as they slid into Deadwood with their stone-boat. It was hard for them to believe that a year earlier this narrow valley with steep hills rising from the valley floor contained only a mountain stream and a few wild animals. The valley was now filled with hastily built buildings, shops, hotels, saloons, offices, warehouses and whorehouses. Most of the buildings were one story tall and made of logs, many of them with ostentatious false fronts, but in the center of the town stood a number of two-story buildings and a three-story hotel built with sawed lumber. More were being built. The valley was only two and ahalf blocks wide at its widest point. Buildings along two dirt roads running parallel to the valley defined the layout of the town. The roads showed no signs of permanency and could be described as a space between buildings filled with obstacles such as logs and other building materials, unintentional ruts that could hold a wagon and trenches that were related to the construction going on. The streets were constantly jammed with wagons and other conveyances and the animals used for pulling them. Adding to the congestion were many young men hurrying along the streets or lounging against the store fronts. There were no walkways to separate the pedestrians from the other traffic so everything was mixed together. It seemed as if a perpetual holiday celebration was taking place. Occasionally a woman could be seen moving down the street with her skirt hiked up to keep it out of the dirt and animal waste.

Karl was amazed to see this hive of human activity. Everyone and everything he saw, except the logs, had to have come in by wagon train since the previous winter. The distance, the Indians, and the army had not done much to deter this logistical miracle.

"Heinrich, I kind of remember you and Pat talking about beating the rush, all those obstacles would slow things down."

"We might have been a little off on that. Think what it would be like without all those hurdles."

The wagon train disassembled, and its members joined this illegal and rapidly growing settlement in the middle of Indian territory.

Karl and Heinrich decided one of the first things to do was try some of the local beer, a beverage that they had not been able to obtain since leaving Sidney, Nebraska. Ben, the fellow that had paid for the privilege of riding on their stone boat, joined them.

It was not difficult to find a saloon. They could see a half a dozen from where they were standing. They picked one, the Hard Rock Saloon, found a table, and ordered a pitcher of beer. They were shocked when they were charged forty cents, more than twice what they were used to paying. Ben picked up a paper laying on one of the chairs, The Black Hills Pioneer. The paper was four pages long, made up of a single large sheet of paper folded in the middle and printed on both sides. The paper stock was a washed-out grey color, the printing uneven but legible. Ben could read English so he started quoting from an article describing the current state of the town. "Population 10,000 men, about 200 women."

Ben read on, "There are businesses opening up every day. At current count there are five hotels, six restaurants, two dance houses, twenty-one grocers, two brewers, one bank, three shoemakers, six bakeries, eleven clothing houses, eight Chinese laundries, one newspaper and twenty-seven saloons."

"Twenty-seven saloons. Think that's enough?" Heinrich wondered.

"Murder and suicides are the main cause of death."

"It says that?" Karl was asking.

"That's what it says."

The newspaper gave the newcomers a quick introduction to the rapidly growing settlement in Indian territory which had no legal status, no laws or legal system, and a population made up primarily of young men from the four corners of the country. Men who were not only young, but who had been willing to walk more than two hundred miles over primitive trails through all kinds of weather and through hostile Indian territory to an uncertain place and situation.

"What does it say about gold?" Karl wanted to know.

"Ya, what about gold?" Heinrich asked. "We came here for gold, not Dead-wood."

"Don't say anything about gold. Guess that's too common to be news."

Karl and Heinrich found a place to park their belongings. They set up their tent in the Badlands, an area downstream from the main part of the town, and where the Chinese and red-light districts were established. It wasn't the fanciest address in town, but for veterans of packing plant and lumberjack accommodations, it would do.

After a couple of days of wandering around Deadwood they decided they needed to get serious about the gold-prospecting thing. Karl arrived in Dead-wood almost broke. Heinrich still had part of his Sidney poker winnings, and he had sold the yoke of oxen for three ounces of gold which was equivalent to sixty dollars. Heinrich volunteered to carry Karl for a while, but cautioned him not to forget the high interest rate.

Karl's concern was that whatever amount they had, it was not going to last long at the prices they were charging in Deadwood. They needed to get started doing what they had come to do.

They started off their prospecting by asked a bartender if he knew anything about staking a claim.

"I know all the best prospects have been claimed up. That's why I'm tending bar."

Heinrich could hardly believe that. "We just heard about the gold this spring, got here about as fast as we could."

"Part of the reason is that they made the claims so damn big. The first people here set up the district and the rules. You might not be surprised to learn that the rules favored the ones who got here first. The claims on the creeks run three hundred feet up and down the stream and rim to rim. That set the pattern. Claims on the hills run about the same size, or bigger. Hell, out in California in forty-nine, claims were one hundred feet on a side. Even if they would have made them one hundred one way, that would still be big and there could have been three times as many claims on the streams. Some latecomers tried to get the rules changed, but they were outgunned. All that's left are hillsides and hilltops where, in most cases, you have to dig down to bedrock and hope you hit lodestone. It's a real long shot. Or you can go panning up some remote creek and hope you can find a new source.

"Another part of the reason is that there are more prospectors than gold. Takes more than hostile Indians and an army to keep the hordes away when they smell gold."

"How do you know what has been claimed?"

"Got to go to the Lost Mining District office, right down the street. They record claims, got a map that shows you what has been claimed and what can be claimed. But I can tell you, all of the best claims are staked."

Karl and Heinrich didn't like what they were hearing. Reality was beginning to obliterate the imagined prospecting that they would be doing.

Karl and Heinrich found the Lost Mining District office housed in a one-room log cabin at the end of the block. There were several people recording claims or getting information when they arrived.

The legal status of the claims office might be in question, operating as it was in Indian territory, but the mining community needed some framework, some means of issuing and recording claims, and the Lost Mining District office had been established by the miners for that purpose.

One wall was covered with a map with recorded claims overdrawn on it. The map confirmed what the bartender had said. Every foot of the creeks and streambeds in the area had been claimed, as had many of the hilltops and hillsides.

The man working in the office finished with the man he had been dealing with and asked if he could help.

"How do you file a claim?" Heinrich asked.

"You are in the right place. Check the map. You can see the areas that are open. Nothing left on the streams. You have to buy them if you want one of those. Otherwise there is a lot of land in the hills you could claim. Generally limited to half an acre. The map is approximate—the stakes you put in the ground are the real boundaries. If you find something, show us what you got and we will register it if hasn't already been claimed. There's a small fee. Need to pay my salary, you know."

"No stream claims left, anywhere?"

"Not around here. Look at it this way. All the creek gold eroded from lodes that are up in the hills, and there is still a lot of land up there to be claimed. Course, the odds of finding gold in those hills is slim. Not like panning in a stream where you can make pretty good wages on average." The clerk smiled and added encouragingly, "but if you hit a lode vein, that's the jackpot."

The facts of the real world were becoming more clear and they didn't exactly reflect the rosy scenario that Heinrich and Pat had described back in the Eau Claire saloon. Karl had never expected that getting to Deadwood would assure them of great riches. He had anticipated working a claim with the possibility of increasing his wherewithal to achieve owning a good piece of farm land in America. Deep in the recesses of his mind, there did lurk the thought that they might end up finding a bonanza that would change everything. Karl suppressed that thought, knowing that it would not be likely. If it happened, he wanted it to surprise him.

They retreated to the Red Rock saloon to contemplate their next move.

They sipped their beer, not saying anything for a time. Heinrich finally broke the silence. "I had thought getting here was the big problem. I don't want to believe that we risked our lives going through Indian country, spending a couple months of our time and a lot of money just for a dollar-a-day job."

"Things are higher here, maybe get two dollars a day."

"*Macht nichts*, same thing."

"You are right, Heinrich, we got to give it a try. I was thinking, maybe we wouldn't hit it rich, but we would be getting something. Like panning, you have some good days and bad ones, but you are almost sure of getting a little gold in a stream where gold has been found. With a dry land claim you are looking for something big, but you might never find it. In the meantime you have to live."

"That's important."

"I've got an idea. If we both search for gold, there is a real good possibility that we would run out of money before we find gold. So what if one of us does the prospecting and the other one gets a job to keep us eating?"

"Not bad. Who does what?"

"We flip a coin. I've a silver dollar."

"I'll call it and name what I get to do if it comes up."

"What will it be?"

"Heads."

Karl flipped the coin. "It's heads. What do you want to do?"

"Guess."

"Prospect."

"You guessed right."

Ben came into the saloon, recognized them, got himself a beer, and pulled up a chair.

Karl asked, "Have you figured this place out? What are you going to be doing?"

"Prospecting, that's what I came here to do. Me and Jim, another fellow that was with the wagon train, are heading into the hills in a couple of days."

The table the men were sitting at had a view of the main street which was filled with men, horses, oxen, wagons coming and going. The previous evening word had spread that Crook City, a town to the east of Deadwood, was under attack by Indians, and a group of locals had gone down to help them out. Some of those men had apparently returned and were standing around in groups, still shouldering long guns.

After a while Karl and Heinrich noticed a lot of commotion outside the window. Someone came in the door and yelled that Wild Bill had been shot. The two men looked at each other. Since when did they start announcing the names of the murdered as it was happening? They had only been here a week, long enough to be aware that murder was one of the major health problems in the town, but people didn't run around announcing each event. Everybody owned a gun and wore it like their boots or their hat. It was part of the normal daily attire. Mix that with a lot of young men and a lot of liquor, and you would have some fatalities, you could bet good money on that.

This had to be something special.

Rumors flew around the saloon tables.

"Killed?"

"Hell yes, shot through the back of his head. He was sitting with his back to the door. You would think he would have been smarter than that."

"What's going on?" Karl wanted to know.

Ben had acquired some knowledge about the local celebrities. "Sounds like somebody shot Wild Bill Hickock."

"So, people get shot around here pretty often from what I hear."

"Ya, but Wild Bill is one of the best known gunslingers in the West."

"Then how come he got shot?" Heinrich wanted to know.

The excitement caused by the Wild Bill shooting was quieting down when the three beer drinkers witnessed yet another scene in the event-filled day.

A dark-skinned Mexican rode down the street holding a short stick with something stuck on the end of it. As he got closer, they could see that it was a head, an Indian head.

"What to hell?" Karl exclaimed.

"Must want to collect the bounty," Ben explained. "They pay a bounty to anyone that brings in an Indian head. Fifty dollars."

For some reason this upset Karl. He was Prussian, a people not known for their good works or piousness, but this seemed a bit much for even a Prussian's sensibilities.

Ben added, "The Indians believe that they have to have a whole body to get to the happy hunting grounds. Without a head, well, you know there is no way."

Heinrich was becoming a little unnerved by all the events unfolding outside the saloon window. "Is this a normal day in Deadwood?"

Ben laughed. "They don't have normal days."

Karl found himself defending the headless Indian. "You can't blame the Indians for being a little pissed. This is supposed to be their land."

"There's gold here." Ben explained. He did not offer additional justification, nor did he feel that he needed to.

Karl understood. Fairness and justice didn't count for much when gold was involved. Gold rules. Although he understood, his mind rebelled at accepting what it perceived to be a great injustice. Karl held these feelings close, knowing that they were not widely shared.

# CHAPTER 24

▼

# GOING SEPARATE WAYS

Heinrich could now devote his time to looking for gold, and he set about doing that.

Meanwhile Karl studied the employment possibilities. There had to be many opportunities. Towns were being built from scratch and there were thousands of men that needed all kinds of things and there was money to pay for them.

He stopped at the Hard Rock Saloon to refresh himself and found himself studying the bartender, who appeared to be about Karl's age. Something seemed awfully familiar about him. Could it be? The bartender had his back turned, washing some glasses. Karl spoke the word, "Flatow." The bartender looked around, puzzled. He looked at the man who had spoken, but could not place him.

"Karl Mueller from Flatow. Do you remember me, Martin?"

"Herr Mueller," Martin exclaimed. "I'll be damned, who would have believed it! I never would have recognized you with that sunburn and full beard."

Yes, it was Martin Meyer, the minister's son from Flatow. If they had been French, they would have embraced and hugged, but being Prussian, they heartily shook hands, slapped each other on the back, and happily conversed in the Flatow dialect. Martin had been in Deadwood since May, having come in with the Gardner wagon train. He had walked all the way from Cheyenne through snow, mud, and dust. He got here early enough to stake a claim on Deadwood Creek, which he worked for a couple of months with fair results, and then traded for the Hard Rock Saloon which was his current source of livelihood.

Martin's father had finally given up the dream of Martin following in his footsteps. He more or less washed his hands of any of Martin's future plans and did not encourage or discourage his plans to go to America.

"Karl, I wasn't cut out for the ministry, so like you I followed the rainbow to America."

Karl wanted to know about the family he had left over five years ago.

"I left two years after you did. They were fine. Your mother moved. She lived with Walter, that is about all I know. Oh, Katrina, I think she got married to some fellow who worked for the baron. I would bet they emigrated. The choice between being a peasant and emigrating is pretty clear."

Karl told Martin his story, what he was doing here, and his plan to eventually homestead some land. "Right now I'm looking for work. My partner is going to look for the pot of gold and I'm going to find a job so we don't starve before we find it."

"Look no further, I could use someone to help me in this place. I know the Muellers are good workers and we can talk Flatow German."

"What would I do? I never worked in a saloon before. Not even close."

"I can teach you what you need to know in half a day. Two dollars a day, seven days a week. Some days long, some days you can take it easy. Try it, we will see how it goes."

"When do I start?"

"How about today? I'll show you a few things you should know. Most of what you need to know you can learn on the job."

"The drinks are whiskey straight, by the bottle or glass; wine, same way; beer is on tap. Prices are on the wall back of the bar."

Martin showed Karl where the fully loaded revolver was always kept, in a drawer right under the cash register. "Don't worry about armed robbery," Martin advised. "It would be a pretty dumb robber who would pull a gun in this town. He would probably get shot down just for sport, but you don't want to be the only unarmed person around."

"There are a few simple rules. If you follow them you will keep from getting into too much trouble.

"Rule one: Don't intervene in personal disputes. Broken furniture can be replaced.

"Rule two: Don't remove rowdy patrons. If they become obnoxious, they will probably get into a fight and rule one will apply.

'Rule three: The bartender does not maintain order. He manages chaos.
'Does that all make sense?"
"I think I get the idea."
"You'll learn. Where are you living?"
"My partner and I have a tent in the Badlands."
Martin wrinkled his nose. "That's not good. I have my apartment upstairs. It has two bedrooms. I would share it with you, but sometimes I have company. There is another one up there not being used. Has a small bedroom, sort of a kitchen-living area. Full of junk right now. Two dollars a week if you want to live up there."
It sounded good to Karl.
And so Karl started his saloon career in Deadwood. He found that bartending in Deadwood, like bartending everywhere, involved a lot of listening to the woes of the down-and-out and the exploits of the boasters. Consoling the down-and-out was a service bartenders were expected to provide as well as maintaining a look of interest when cornered by a bragger. Karl also found that bartending in Deadwood had some unique challenges. First, the clientele was mostly armed young males, and second, there was no legal authority to enforce law and order in the town. This was Indian territory, outside the jurisdiction of the United States government and its laws.

*       *       *       *

Heinrich had disappeared into the hills west of Deadwood, but kept Karl informed of his efforts when he came back to town for supplies a couple of times a month. He would make use of Karl's apartment when he was in town.
Heinrich had settled on a piece of land on a steep slope that lay between a dry-land claim that was paying out near the top of a ridge and a gold-bearing stream below it. He applied for two claims, one in Karl's name and one in his. The two claims took up a good part of the slope between the paying dirt on top and the creek below.
The claim was on land that sloped at a 45-degree angle, so Heinrich had to create a flat surface by digging into the hill and using the excavated dirt to build a platform where he constructed a one-room cabin, ten by twelve feet in size.
Heinrich had determined that the bedrock under the claim was made up of seams that exposed the layered history of the bedrock. He began working on an ambitious plan that he figured would reveal any gold that might be hidden under the overburden that covered the claim. He would dig down to bedrock and make

a trench from the bottom to the top of the claim that bisected the seams in the bedrock. In that way he would be able to examine every layer in the bedrock that lay under the claim. The overburden varied in depth. He hit bedrock four feet down in one spot and had not found it after going down twelve feet in another place. Complicating the task were the trees that covered the claim and large loose boulders mixed in the overburden. Heinrich expected the project would take him well into the next year. He didn't dwell on the possibility that he wouldn't find gold. With gold outcrops above him and gold in the creek below, he was optimistic.

*     *     *     *

Karl soon adapted to his new work. It was not as physically demanding as the kind of work he was used to, but it was demanding in other ways and the hours were long. Karl learned that thinking on his feet and putting up with some really obnoxious characters was part of the job. You never knew who was going to walk in the door or how they were going to act.

Karl found that Martin's rules worked well. Don't confront a drunk prospector. Guide them in the direction you wanted them to go, and it usually worked.

One evening a particularly obnoxious cowboy was acting up. The cowboy was dressed in buckskin, topped off with a Stetson hat, and packed a revolver in a holster that hung on a filled cartridge belt. He was clean shaven with shoulder-length hair. He told outlandish stories, loud enough for just about everyone in the place to hear. Well-oiled before arriving, he proceeded to get skunk drunk and started yelling like a wounded coyote. Karl was expecting rule one to kick in, but the other patrons seemed to tolerate what would normally have set one or two of them off by this time.

A regular was sitting at the bar and Karl queried him about the indifference to the really bad behavior being exhibited.

"Oh hell, that's Calamity Jane. People just kinda put up with her. Like the Queen of England, she can't do any wrong. She will probably pass out pretty soon. Someone will help her home."

Calamity Jane apparently caught a whiff of Karl's conversation. She staggered behind the bar, "You God damn right, Calamity Jane, you little runt—let me plant a big damn kiss on you," and she fell against Karl, who drew back because the body odor was pretty bad, causing her to fold up and fall to the floor behind the bar. Two locals volunteered to take her home.

And so Karl was introduced to Deadwood's most famous female resident during the summer of 1876. She had arrived in June with the Colorado Charlie Utter wagon train that originated in Cheyenne, along with around 190 gold seekers, including a couple of wagon loads of queens, the first girls to arrive. Calamity Jane had worked as an outrider for the wagon train.

As time went on Karl found that his duties at the Hard Rock Saloon expanding as Martin entrusted him with more and more responsibilities. After a month or two, his title might have been manager, except that he didn't have the authority or pay to go with the responsibility.

While Karl was taking over many of Martin's tasks, Martin was not idle. He was doing a lot of wheeling and dealing, mostly in real estate. He bought another saloon in town, which he started managing, and in addition he gambled regularly, often for high stakes, and drank heavily. Gambling and heavy drinking did not make one stand out in Deadwood; on the contrary, Martin blended in well.

The new saloon and Martin's other activities monopolized his time and he eventually recognized the need for somebody to officially do what Karl was already doing—manage the Hard Rock Saloon.

Once Martin recognized the problem, he set about resolving it. "Karl, I'm going to make you manager of the Hard Rock. I know you been doing that, but I'm going to make it official, so the help will know who's the boss."

"What about the pay?"

"Job's the same. I'm just going to make it official."

"For what I am being paid, I can go next door, tend bar, and not worry about all that management stuff."

"Karl, I took you off the street, fed you, gave you shelter."

"I'll be forever grateful."

"But you want more money?"

"Like I said."

"How about three dollars a day?"

Karl put out his hand. "Fair enough."

"Oh, and I won't be using the upstairs apartment anymore. You can move in there if you want, rent will be part of your pay."

"That's even fairer."

"One thing you should know. Now that you are an official manager, you have to think different.

"You said nothing but the title changed, and I get a dollar a day more. Now you want me to think different?"

"Well, you can manage a business and not know what you are doing, but it is time that you know what businesses are for. Do you know why there is a Hard Rock Saloon?

"To make money?"

"Close, but not quite right. More exactly, what you want to make is a profit. The only reason for a business to exist is to make a profit. Every society has a system that guides the way it does things. In Prussia the system is a leftover from the feudal days. Power comes first, and from it wealth. In America it is a capitalistic system. In it, profit comes first, then wealth, and from it comes power. It is getting to the same thing from a different direction. Power and wealth are the same thing, they are equal. So remember, profit, wealth, power.

"And here are some rules to remember:

"Rule one, you run a business to make a profit. You don't run a saloon so people have a place to drink, or a shoe shop to fix shoes, or a grocery store so people have something to eat. You run every business for the same thing: Profit.

"Rule two, don't mix your personal concerns or sensibilities with the purpose of a business. You don't hire people because they need a job, or because they are your friend or relative. You hire them to help the business make a profit. Don't pay any more for anything than you have to. The purpose of a business is not to heal the sick or help the poor. It took me a while to figure that out, being that my father was a minister, and to him, doing good, ministering to the sick and poor, was what it was all about. A business doesn't concern itself with that kind of stuff, unless you can make a profit from doing it.

"Rule three, don't mix business and pleasure, unless it helps the bottom line, and it usually doesn't."

"I don't know if I understand all of that," Karl replied. "Does it have anything to do with trying to get me to work as manager with no raise in pay?"

"That's it. You already know most of what a manager needs to know."

*    *    *    *

The Hard Rock was a small saloon by Deadwood standards. It had a bar and a dozen tables for sitting and drinking or private gambling, and two faro tables in the back. A single bartender worked the bar full-time; a second bartender was behind the bar in busy periods. Another one roamed the tables, fetched drinks, and picked up. The bar normally had four to six women who would sit with customers for tips and drinks. They were called happy girls. These women weren't paid directly by the saloon. They were independent contractors so to speak, which meant they were allowed to use the premises for the business they would draw and for a split of the proceeds for any drink ordered for them or the party they were with. These women did some hustling, but the Hard Rock Saloon did not get involved in that part of it. The saloon selected the women who could operate on its premises, and any that didn't belong were moved along. The dealers at the faro tables were also independent operators, paying the saloon a fee for the use of the tables. Regular customers often gambled on their own at saloon tables at no cost.

One thing that soon became obvious to Karl was that being recognized as a saloon manager had some peripheral benefits.

A woman that came in one day made him fully aware of his status change. She wanted to be one of the saloon's happy girls—she was looking for a spot to roost.

When she came in one afternoon, her bosom was one of the first things Karl noticed about her. She attained the "hourglass look" honestly.

"Karl, I hear you are the big cheese here now. So I got to ask you. Are you needing any girls for your tables?"

"Well, we got six on the list now. That is the most we carry. They come and go. Come by once in a while and check."

"I like your accent. I really need something now. Is there anything I could do to get on the list. You know, for you personally?"

There were times in the recent past when Karl would have walked straight up the wall to accommodate this woman's needs, but for one thing, his libido had slowed down a tick or two, and for another thing, one of Martin's rules warned him about mixing business and pleasure.

"You would brighten the place up, that's for sure, but we have to draw the line somewhere. You probably go by here a couple of times a day. Stop in. If you want, I'll put your name on the list, and you will get the next spot that comes up."

"Sally is the name. Can you remember my face?

"That and more."

Sometimes things happen that are unplanned, unexplainable, and improbable. Ana was one of those things.

Ana had come in with the Garner wagon train, the same as Martin. Her name hinted at Mexican ancestry, which would explain her dark skin. She was a beauty, with dark eyes and hair to go with her tawny skin color. Her body was small, well-proportioned. Her pretty face had slightly pronounced cheek bones. If you could coax a smile out of her, a mouth full of straight white teeth would be revealed.

safe distance and the fuze was list. There was a horrendous explosion. One side of the bank building was blown out, and the steel plates designed to contain the blast were thrown about two hundred feet. After the smoke cleared, the sheriff and the blasting crew went in to assess the results. The safe had been blown over on its back, but the safe door was firmly in place. On closer inspection, they noticed that the safe door, though firmly closed, had been sprung a little bit. They were able to get a pry bar into one corner and enlarge the opening a little bit more. Blasting powder was poured into the opening. One of the steel plates was strapped on top of the safe to direct the charge. The result was a minor explosion when compared to the first blast, but there was enough force to spring the safe door a little more. A third charge sprung the safe door wide open. The sheriff had everyone stand back while he checked the contents of the safe. He came up with a handful of paper but no money.

Karl and Ana had been observing all of this activity for most of the morning. Karl's original concerns about having lost the money he had deposited were pretty well confirmed. He was wondering if he had the strength and the will to continue to pursue his dream. He had faced many setbacks, but this one seemed to suck the strength out of his body.

After the excitement at the bank began to dissipate, Karl started thinking about what to do next.

Ana resolved the problem with a question. "Don't you think we should get going? We can still make some distance today."

"Go where?" Karl asked.

Ana acted surprised, "Ortonville. That is where we are going. Isn't it?"

"Do you understand what has happened?" he asked.

"It will mean we will have a little less money," she replied.

Ana reached over to Karl and took his hand. "We will have a little less money, nothing else has changed. We will find a way to live your dream without it."

Ana's downplaying the seriousness of the problem did relieve Karl's self-guilt. Karl had made a bad decision. Hindsight made that clear. He did have concerns about the viability of the bank, and despite those concerns, went ahead and did it. Ana had every right to be disturbed, but she wasn't. And she was right, they had to continue down the path they were going, there was really no other choice.

Karl talked to the sheriff, showing him his deposit information. The sheriff told Karl to send his address when he settled down. If there was a recovery, the sheriff would contact Karl.

"Don't hold your breath," the sheriff advised Karl.

# CHAPTER 28

▼

# THE LAST STEP

In the middle of the afternoon, Karl and Ana took a ferry boat to the east bank of the Missouri. Heinrich's horse, carrying some of their extra baggage, was tethered to Karl's horse.

Karl had laid out the route on a map that showed little besides blank space between Fort Pierre and Ortonville. It did show some rivers and lakes, but there were no known trails or settlements. The route he laid out was a straight line between the end points. They would be traveling through a sea of grass with few defined landmarks and would depend on the sun and a compass to stay on track.

They expected the trip to be uneventful. They would no longer be in Indian territory, the terrain was flat or gently rolling, and there were no major physical obstacles. Karl estimated that at a moderate pace, it would take three or four days to cover the distance. The weather was unpredictable at this time of the year and could range from warm and dry to wet and cold.

Ana was aware that Karl was deeply troubled by the loss of the money he had deposited in the bank. He was not the optimistic, cheerful Karl that she was used to. As they crossed on the ferry she tried to reassure him. "Everything will be alright. I know it. In no time we will have made up for what we lost."

Karl tried to respond to her optimism but found it was difficult.

The weather was promising as they headed into the bluffs east of the Missouri River. The afternoon sun was shining, and a cool wind blew briskly from the northwest. There were large rolling hills and deep gullies and ravines near the river, but the terrain started to level out as they moved further east.

They were moving towards their intended destination, which was both a spot on the map and the place where the dream that had been driving Karl for over seven years was to be fulfilled. With the loss of the majority of Karl's savings, there were now questions and doubts about how that dream would be accomplished. Karl would not have the resources to make a homestead productive in the short term. Maybe he could homestead some land and find work to keep things going until the homestead was developed. These thoughts were going through Karl's mind as they rode into the endless grass horizon.

As they proceeded, Karl's spirits began to improve. The brisk clear air, the feel of a good horse moving under the saddle, and the boundless prairie vistas were like a tonic. He glanced over at Ana riding beside him. She rode straight in the saddle with her head held high. There were no signs of worry or concern on her face. It was hard to remain troubled and unhappy in this setting. He moved his horse over next to Ana's, took her hand and held it for a long moment. Ana, squeezed Karl's hand in response and smiled.

As the distance from Fort Pierre increased, it became easier for Karl to assess the impact of the loss of most of the money he had accumulated. He was beginning to appreciate Ana's assessment of the matter. All that had changed was that they had a little less money.

Karl and Ana made camp by a small creek that night. It was running fast and clear with the spring runoff. Grass was growing right down to the edge of the rippling stream, and scattered willows outlined its path.

The horses were unsaddled, given a drink and tethered. They could find more than they could eat at their feet in this thick prairie. Karl found enough old, dead willow branches to make a fire. The sun reached the horizon while they prepared the evening meal, and the sky took on a red glow that stretched north to south to the edges of the earth, and up above until the color was absorbed by the approaching night. Karl and Ana took it in and were sure that this had to be one of the earth's most beautiful places.

They let the fire die down early, and the clear moonless night settled in upon them. They sat on their bedrolls and watched the stars thicken into what appeared to be a three-dimensional picture, with many bright stars and planets pressing down near where they sat, while dimmer stars receded out into space. Occasionally they saw a flash. Karl called them shooting stars. Heavenly fireworks with no sound. A duck in the nearby stream quacked, otherwise the stillness of the night was complete.

They had combined their bedrolls and lay in each other's arms, savoring each other in the darkness.

The following morning a menagerie of birds announced the coming of a new day, and they were soon underway. It was another sunny day with the wind shifting more to the north, keeping the air cool. Another good day for riding.

This land, which had only recently been a primary range for the buffalo, seemed devoid of large animals. Skeletal remains scattered here and there was the only evidence once massive buffalo herds. Occasionally they would see a flighty herd of antelope and a coyote slinking about. Large jackrabbits would bound away when disturbed. They saw large numbers of birds migrating north to their summer nesting areas. Prairie stretched to the horizon in every direction. The land, appeared huge and devoid of human habitants.

The composition of the land changed from low rolling hills to an absolutely flat prairie over the course of the day. Looking at his map, Karl determined that this must be the James River Valley. The map indicated a small river, but apparently one that ran through a wide flat valley. At midday they came upon the river itself. It was high, with water running out of the rivers banks.due to the spring snow melt.

They stopped at the water's edge.

"What do you think?" Karl asked.

"It looks like we swim."

"Maybe we could find a fordable spot somewhere along the river."

"Not likely with the water this high."

"Do you know how to swim? I don't."

"It don't matter. Horses know how."

"You sure?"

"All horses know how to swim. Even horses that have never put their hoofs in water."

Karl waded into the stream. It was cold. He found the bottom receded sharply and was soon up to his armpits in icy water.

"Brr—that's cold. Looks like we are going to find out if you are right about horses knowing how to swim."

The gear they were carrying was re-packed, putting it as high on the horses as possible.

Karl looked at Ana, "Any special instructions?"

"Walk the horses into the water, and when you get into deep water hold onto the saddle horn, you just float along once the horse starts swimming." Then, without hesitating, Ana led her horse into the river. "This water is cold!" she exclaimed.

The horse, although reluctant, let Ana lead her into the deep water and was soon swimming, with Ana floating along its side. In a short time they had gained the opposite bank of the river.

Karl followed suit and led his gelding into the water. The horse pulled back on the lines, not sure this was a good idea, but then, trusting that Karl knew what he was doing, continued to move into the stream. The trailing horse followed without protest. When the gelding felt the bottom fall away, it began moving its legs as though running, and it discovered a natural ability to swim. Karl floated alongside the horse and held onto the saddle horn. He encouraged the animal, though it needed little since the only land visible to its eyes was the far shore, and it swam towards it with all of its might. They were soon back on land. Karl was wet and shivering, but otherwise undamaged from the swim in the cold river.

They stripped off their cloths and changed into something dry. The horses, better equipped, only had to shake themselves to get rid of the water in their coats.

"You were right, Ana. They all know how to swim."

"You didn't believe?"

"Well, when you feel that bottom drop away, and you know you can't swim, it does test your faith."

They rode the rest of the day on flat land, and the prairie grass seemed to get denser and taller as they proceeded in an easterly direction. This was definitely plow country. Towards evening, hills appeared, and the land started to slope upward. They had reached the east edge of the James River Valley.

The next day they were rode through rolling hills with many small ponds and sloughs scattered about. It was still a prairie from horizon to horizon, but the composition of the landscape had changed. It was their third day of travel, and they had not seen another human or a human settlement since they left the Missouri River. It was eerie. This obviously fertile, arable land was sitting, just waiting for man to put it to better use.

Karl mentioned this to Ana, that it seemed like the land was being wasted.

"But so pretty," she replied.

"Fields of grain can be pretty too."

"That's true."

Ana's concern was real. Soon it would no longer look like this. It would be forever changed, like the forest in Wisconsin. Karl understood her concern, but it was his dream to tame a patch of this land. He would make it more beautiful than it now was. He believed he could do that.

As the day progressed, the hills became steeper, with more sloughs, lakes, and deep ravines. This was quite picturesque and a relief after the flat James River Valley, but Karl was becoming concerned since they were approaching their destination, and turning this terrain into productive farm land might be a challenge.

The wind veered around to the southwest, and the temperature was rising and very comfortable as Karl and Ana neared the end of their third day of travel. They had begun looking for a likely spot to spend their last night on the trail when they came onto the brow of a hill from which a panorama of a flat valley stretched out as far as they could see.

Karl was transfixed. He could finally see the end of his long jouney. Somewhere in that valley they would find land—a home. Exactly how that was going to be accomplished was still to be determined and could be difficult, but the past few days had restored his confidence that he, together with Ana, could overcome any obstacles they might encounter.

They decided they should spend the night right there, at that spot, where they could view the valley as they prepared the evening meal and set up camp.

The next morning they were up early and started the descent into the valley where they would complete the journey—together.

0-595-31590-9

Printed in the United States
46507LVS00004B/1-102

9 780595 315901